APOCALYPTIC FICTION FROM PERMUTED PRESS

"[*THUNDER AND ASHES*] IS A TIGHT AND ENGAGING ADDITION TO THE ZOMBIE GENRE THAT FANS SHOULD DEFINITELY ADD TO THEIR COLLECTION."
—LEAH CLARKE, FLAMESRISING.COM

EMPIRE: "A macabre masterpiece of post-apocalyptic zombie goodness."
—Dr. Pus, *Library of the Living Dead*

HEADSHOT QUARTET: "One hell of a collection and deserves a place on your shelf..."
—Shawn Rutledge, SkullRing.org

HISTORY IS DEAD: "A violent and bloody tour through the ages... simultaneously mind-numbingly savage and thought provoking."
—Michael McBride, author of *Species*

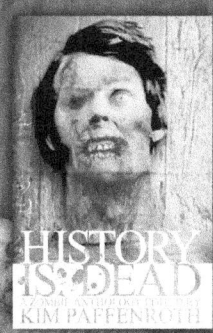

AVAILABLE AT AMAZON.COM, BN.COM, MOST ONLINE BOOKSTORES, OR ASK YOUR LOCAL BOOKSELLER
HTTP://WWW.PERMUTEDPRESS.COM

Weird Tales®

WEIRD TALES was the *first* storytelling magazine devoted explicitly to the realm of the **dark and fantastic.**

Founded in 1923, WEIRD TALES provided a literary home for such diverse wielders of the imagination as **H.P. Lovecraft** (creator of Cthulhu), **Robert E. Howard** (creator of Conan the Barbarian), **Margaret Brundage** (artistic godmother of goth fetishism), and **Ray Bradbury** (author of *The Illustrated Man* and *Something Wicked This Way Comes*).

Today, O wondrous reader of the 21st century, we continue to seek out that which is most weird and unsettling, for your own edification and alarm.

FICTION

INTERNATIONAL AUTHOR SPOTLIGHT

FIRST PHOTOGRAPH | Zoran Živković **20**
Sometimes the dominant twin is the silent one.

THE GONG | Sara Genge **24**
Across the battlefield, one eunuch envied the maidens.

THE DREAM OF THE BLUE MAN | Nir Yaniv **36**
Mystery slept in the shadow of the skyscraper.

THE WORDEATERS | Rochita Loenen-Ruiz **42**
The child was magical. *Too* magical.

OUT OF SACRED WATER | Juraj Červeňák **48**
One sorcerer. One war brigade. One ancient forest.

TIME AND THE ORPHEUS | chiles samaniego **62**
An ex-pirate's nightclub hosts a singular horn player.

BLEAKWARRIOR MEETS THE SONS OF BRAWL **70**
Alistair Rennie | The metadimensional streetfighting throwdown of the year.

EXCLUSIVE NOVEL EXCERPT!

THE ALCHEMY OF STONE | Ekaterina Sedia **86**
A clockwork girl, emo gargoyles, and a city in turmoil.

EDITORIAL & CREATIVE DIRECTOR Stephen H. Segal FICTION EDITOR Ann VanderMeer
CONTRIBUTING EDITORS Amanda Gannon, Elizabeth Genco, Kenneth Hite, Darrell Schweitzer
EDITOR EMERITUS George H. Scithers EDITORIAL ASSISTANTS Colin Azariah-Kribbs,
Tessa Kum CONTRIBUTING ARTISTS Steven Archer, Adrian Costea,
Hellstern, Pavel Lagutin, Ira Marcks, Scott Maxwell, Joy Prescott

PUBLISHER John Gregory Betancourt
ADVERTISING SALES Evelyn Kriete ASSISTANT TO THE PUBLISHER Renee Farrah

All writers of such stories are prophets

FEATURES

14 Viktor Koen's Biomechanical Visions
What happens when a classically trained Greek artist
enters the digital-mashup millennium?

81 The Weird Films of Bill Plympton
His dreamlike animated tales have lit up countless screens.
Bill Plympton talks in depth about the creative process.

POETRY

13 | THE MONSTER WITH THE SHAPE OF ME
Brian J. Hatcher

DEPARTMENTS

4 | THE EYRIE | weirdness in many languages
6 | WEIRDISM | the apocalypse will be cinematographized
8 | THE LIBRARY | monsters, ghosts and more Halloween reading
10 | THE BAZAAR | steampunk beasts and a plethora of skulls
12 | HARVEY PELICAN & CO. | special offers from the esoterica king
92 | LOST IN LOVECRAFT | Kenneth Hite finds Cthulhu in the Pacific

COVER ILLUSTRATION **| Viktor Koen**

VOL. 63, NO. 4 **| Issue 351**

WEIRD TALES ® is published 6 times a
year by Wildside Press, LLC. Postmaster
and others: send all changes of address
and other subscription matters to Wildside Press, 9710 Traville Gateway Dr.
#234, Rockville MD 20850–7408. Single
copies, $6.99 in U.S.A. & possessions; $10
by first class mail elsewhere. Subscrip-
tions: 6 issues $24 in U.S.A. & posses-
sions; $45 elsewhere, in U.S. funds.
Single-copy orders should be addressed to
WEIRD TALES at the address above.
Copyright © 2008 by Wildside Press, LLC.
All rights reserved; reproduction prohib-
ited without prior permission. Typeset &
printed in the United States of America.
WEIRD TALES ® is a registered trade-
mark owned by Weird Tales, Limited.

The eyrie

A World Full of Weird Stories

BY ANN VANDERMEER

In my hands I am holding the latest book from author Leena Krohn: *Kotini on Riioraa*. Unfortunately, it is in Finnish, so while I can admire its beautiful, lavish illustrations, I cannot read it.

I mention this because I had the good fortune to not only meet Leena, but also be invited to her home to share a meal with her and her husband Mikael Böök, while visiting Europe a few years ago. That trip was a true revelation to me. I had the opportunity to meet and spend time with so many wonderful people: writers, editors, artists, and readers. Seven countries in five weeks. And delicious books everywhere I looked—but I couldn't partake! Alas, I am only proficient in English, although in my childhood I could converse in three languages.

Then last year I attended the Utopiales conference in Nantes, France, and spent some time with Jim and Kathy Morrow, who had just released their anthology of overseas science fiction, *The SFWA European Hall of Fame*. We talked for hours that week about the tragedy of Americans missing out on such great stories because we limit ourselves to English.

A reoccurring, if utopian, wish came up again and again: *If only we could all speak the same language.* Then all our fiction could be shared seamlessly—and without huge costs. One of the reasons we don't see much in the way of great new translated fiction is that sometimes the translation can cost even more than what the original writer earns. This makes translation projects cost-prohibitive and publishers reluctant to take the chance. It also deprives us of fantastic work we could be enjoying. That's a damn shame.

The Morrows and I also talked about the differences in fiction around the world; how each country has its own flavor of imaginative storytelling. This led me to think a lot about how great it would be to bring more international fiction to an English-speaking audience. And *that* led to this special issue of *Weird Tales,* wherein *all* the fiction is from overseas writers.

(In acquiring the stories for this issue, I discovered more wonderfulness than I could fit in one magazine. So rest assured, *Weird Tales* will be bringing you many more international stories in the future.)

Before introducing the tales in this issue, I'd like to take a moment to recognize those remarkable bilingual writers who have dedicated their time to crafting high-quality translations of other authors' work. Their efforts go largely unnoticed and unrecognized—yet what they do is so very important. While some of the stories appearing in this issue were originally written in English, others were not, and thus I raise my glass to Daren Bakker, Lavie Tidhar, and Alice Copple-Tošić, who've brought their joys to us.

In this issue you will find Slovakian fantasy in the form of a mythic and legendary tale from Juraj Červeňák. You'll discover strange dreamscapes from an even stranger Israel of the future by Nir Yaniv. Come share an exploration of what happens when words are physical things, in a story from Rochita Loenen-Ruiz, a writer originally from the Phillipines, dwelling now in The Netherlands.

Do you know what eunuchs are like in battle? Sarah Genge of Spain shows us. And Serbian writer Zoran Živković unveils what lies unseen in a photo.

What exactly is a Meta-Warrior and why are they so distressed? We find out from Alistair Rennie, a Scottish writer living in Italy. And we are blessed with music that reaches far beyond the boundaries of language from Chiles Samaniego, originally from the Philippines but currently residing in Singapore.

Enjoy. Then go and seek more. ❧

APOCALYPSE RIGHT NOW

How Hollywood learned to stop worrying and love the end of the world

I RECENTLY RAN INTO my friend Patrick, an actor friend in Pittsburgh, who was bummed because he'd been turned down for a role in *The Road*. "They said I wasn't skinny enough," he said. "It's this post-apocalyptic movie, so everybody has to look emaciated, like they haven't eaten in weeks."

It's a morbid thing, this casting call for anemic extras. The joke around Pittsburgh is that John Hillcoat, director of *The Road*, looked high and low for a real post-apocalyptic shooting location—and found one. Based on Cormac McCarthy's Pulitzer Prize-winning novel, *The Road* concerns two survivors of an unnamed holocaust, a father and son who wander the blasted countryside, avoiding cannibals.

But *The Road* is only the latest in a macabre new genre: The World is Screwed Cinema. We've already seen Clive Owen wandering through the tattered ruins of Britain, where armed savages ambush cars in the forest, and nobody can procreate, so life is deprived of meaning. But at least *Children of Men* still claimed a city full of living humans. *I Am Legend* is a solo show, with Will Smith picking through the empty superstructures of New York, tough and savvy but completely alone.

What's this new obsession with annihilation? Why are we drawn to the nightmarish visions of *Cloverfield*, where Manhattan is reduced to grimy tunnels and half-collapsed towers? What fears have inspired the film version of Jose Saramago's *Blindness*, where an unknown sickness blights our eyesight, or *The Happening*, where masses of people just start killing themselves?

These are disturbing predictions, surely, but what's more disturbing is the mystery that lies at the heart of each film: We don't know where the *Cloverfield* monster came from. Nobody can explain the impotent world of *Children of Men*. Even Spielberg's *War of the Worlds* was filmed in intimate close-up; we know the Martians have invaded, but we have no idea why or what they're doing, aside from wiping us out. There is no omniscient narrator in these newer films, no "ah-ha" moment, like in *Independence Day*. These are not morality tales; they are experiments in total nihilism, where unexplained disasters destroy everything we know and love, but life (if you can call it life) torturously slogs on.

There have always been Armageddon stories, and humanity has always been preoccupied with its own destruction. But in the past half-century, our biggest fear has been nuclear catastrophe: cities razed by missiles, the survivors slowly wilted by radiation. Now, post-Cold War and post-September 11, the idea of Mutual Assured Destruction is a little passé. Our anxieties are a little more primal; anybody could be a terrorist, anybody could be in cahoots with terrorists, and meanwhile we still have the pedestrian fears of gangs and viruses and serial killers. (*Psycho* made us afraid to stay in scary hotels, but *Funny Games* makes us terrified to even open the front door.)

And then there's this sudden fear of lost resources. How long will petroleum fuel our civilization? How vulnerable are we to environmental disaster? How much like the late Roman Empire is our decadent lifestyle? Even *Idiocracy* offers a frightening vision—a world of morons eating raw Crisco and watching porn all day, oblivious to its Himalayan landfills. In all these films, humanity is too

naïve, too comfortable, to anticipate its own demise. In *The Road*, McCarthy kills off even the world's plants, leaving only a scatter of mushrooms.

Unlike earlier apocalypse films, our latest movies have the benefit of eye-popping CGI, making our future miseries all the more vivid. *Tank Girl* and *Omega Man* were violent, but they were also incredibly silly. The *Mad Max* films were well-shot, but they took place in a barren desert. In contrast to the Australian Outback, London and New York are familiar cities, and watching Will Smith wander through a rubble-strewn Times Square makes the anarchy much more personal. *Invasion of the Body Snatchers* was scary, but *The Invasion*'s advanced cinematography and A-list actors make the story look as realistic as a documentary. (Directors take note: If you want to make the future look scary, just hire Julianne Moore or Nicole Kidman. Redheads apparently sell disaster). You want to see escaped zoo animals lurking in a shattered office tower? Hollywood can do that.

The question is not where these anxieties come from; the world is faster and more uncertain than ever, and our fears of plagues and suitcase bombs and city-destroying weather patterns are certainly well founded. The real question is this: Are we making these films to warn ourselves about near-future calamity, or are we just resigning ourselves to chaos? In other words, do we still believe we can do something to *prevent* all the death and cannibalism? Just how fucked are we?

The genre's weirdest twist is that it's both cynical and hopeful at the same time: Cynical, because the future is awful, but hopeful, because we can expect some shred of life to continue. A telling tagline comes from a *Children of Men* movie poster: "In 20 years, women are infertile. No children. No future. No hope." Then it adds: "But all that can change in a heartbeat." Sure, death is a random and inevitable event (one major character is unexpectedly shot in the throat; another bludgeons a man's head with a rock), but there are still heroes. These heroes are smart and resourceful, and they're basically good people trapped in horrific circumstances. *Cloverfield*'s New York slackers are really nice kids, and they find love and purpose before getting crushed by a giant space monster. Life sucks and then you die, but at least there's some nobility woven in.

American cinema is always criticized for its unwillingness to allow an unhappy ending. Now that Hollywood is on a roll manufacturing portents of universal doom, we get to see ourselves obliterated by a dozen different cataclysms. So what are we supposed to do with these prophecies? Treat them like any other fictional story? Weigh the pros and cons of our imbalanced world? Or just start believing that, yes, the end is nigh? Because at last, we're getting a pretty good idea of what that nigh end looks like. ☉

Robert Isenberg is a writer and actor based in Pittsburgh.

The Library

Interview | BY ELIZABETH GENCO

LAUREN GROFF: Word Hoarder

Five questions for the author of THE MONSTERS OF TEMPLETON

O ne of the weird literary hits of 2008 is Lauren Groff's novel The Monsters of Templeton, *in which a dead sea-beast interrupts the life of a young woman questing for her father's identity. Stephen King raved over it; we talked with Groff about writing it.*

In one of your interviews, you mention that you "write full drafts, then throw them out completely, and start anew." Is that as horrifying as it sounds? It does sound terrifying, but it wasn't so extremely bad—what breakdowns I had were mostly manageable. The write-and-toss process came about from the project of *Monsters* itself, actually. That's what usually happens, depending on what I'm attempting to do. For example, most of my short stories live in my head for years and years before they're ready to pop out, fully formed, and I only do small modifications before they're ready to go. Novels are different because they're far too large to live in their entirety in my brain.

My two (awful) previous novels, which will never see the light of day, were all written in excessively different manners: the postmodern, fragmented tale was written on index cards and shuffled to make some kind of order; the straightforward story massively over-influenced by Gabriel Garcia Marquez was written from beginning to end in a white heat. Because I had always wanted to make *Monsters* a layered, broad tale spanning centuries, it just so happened that I had to write three complete drafts and throw them away before I found the final, fourth, structure that would make all those layers work together. I do end up keeping some things . . . But mostly, I just try to write from what I remember, which makes the memories better than they are.

What was going on in your life when you began writing *Monsters?* I was twenty-four, and had just thrown out my second novel and was living in California. I'd had a series of horrendous jobs after college—I was the world's worst bartender, temp, canvasser, caseworker and administrative assistant—and I would run home after work to write until my then-boyfriend came home for dinner. I'd also write during my lunch break and, during slow times, at work itself (once or twice prompting shockingly unwelcome commentary from some computer-administrative god who could see everything on my screen). I guess I could have been accused of stealing "company time." One of the temp agencies where I worked in Boston the summer before graduation had previously had Elizabeth Wurtzel in my exact temping position, and apparently she was a time-stealer, too, so it wasn't just me . . . Writing this obsessively was a way, I think, to stave off despair. After the previous novel, which abjectly failed, I decided that I needed to write about something I loved so deeply that I would see through as many drafts as I needed to until it was completed.

Do you write for yourself, or do you have a particular audience in mind? Overall, the first drafts are definitely written for me—they're so horrendous nobody else would want to read them. Then, in massive revision or rewriting I tend to picture a kindly, cheery, exuberant yet intimidatingly smart little fellow who has the ability to turn nasty when I strike a false note or make a logical error, *a la* Bilbo Baggins when he's feeling greedy about the Ring. In graduate school, I wrote my short stories for Lorrie Moore, who was my advisor, and though she was only kind and wise, it was awfully intimidating. Whatever I do, I can't picture my family, because that would kill every artistic impulse I'd have. It's my greatest fear to shame them, and I have to pretend they don't exist to get any writing done at all.

Many of the pictures in the book are from your personal collection of antique photos. Collecting seems to be such a writerly habit; do you collect anything else? I have a very long list of beautiful words, and have a collection of books that is threatening to go through my office floor at the moment. And I love plants—my garden is tiny but full of native Florida specimens that I love more than I love most people.

Name five of your favorite words. After I wrote these, I realized I liked all of them because they created very clear images in my head: *Hirsute*, because I imagine a hair-suit every time. And that makes me laugh. *Fritillary*, a kind of butterfly, because it evokes exactly the kind of movement a butterfly makes. *Lapidary*, a word as smooth and gemlike as whatever it describes. *Ondine*, a kind of naughty water-nymph, which, because I feel most alive in water, makes me happy. And the French word *coquelicot*, which means poppy, because it so perfectly evokes the cheery little red flowers, millions to a field, that once so astonished me with beauty I fell off my (moving) bicycle. ℮

Halloween Book Picks

THE GHOST QUARTET edited by Marvin Kaye (Tor, hardcover, $24.95) • It's natural for ghost stories to channel the past and echo the mythic patterns of folklore, for the ghost itself is an echo of the recognizable past. The customary stereotypes are a part of the genre's comfort zone for readers—but not in *The Ghost Quartet*, where the chilling subversion of genre conventions will knock a traditional horror fan right out of his Victorian armchair and slippers. Brian Lumley's "The Place of Waiting" spirits us away to the Scottish highlands, a favorite locale of phantoms; but few readers will have met the betrayed, vengeful creature that preys upon the protagonist as he struggles to recover from a terrible loss of his own.

"Strindberg's Ghost" by Tanith Lee offers us the familiar motif of a supernaturally lovely spectre, but turns the cliché on its head by portraying a ghost who, rather than fatally enticing her victims, is herself held prisoner by the needy mortals who feed off her presence. Marvin Kaye's "The Haunted Single Malt" concerns friends who are engaged in the time-honored pastime of ghostly storytelling when a disturbing stranger brings them closer than they want to the ethereal world. Finally, Orson Scott Card unsettles us further by ushering in "Hamlet's Ghost," whose hideous secret will catch even the most jaded Shakespearean off guard. *The Ghost Quartet* contains all the wonder and terror of a vividly familiar nightmare—but expect more than a few of its lurking denizens to create nightmares of their own long after their tales are told. —*Colin Azariah-Kribbs*

LOCKE & KEY: WELCOME TO LOVECRAFT by Joe Hill & Gabriel Rodriguez (IDW, hardcover, $24.99) • Their father's brutal murder by a young schoolmate sends three kids to seek sanctuary in the mysterious old family estate—where a special doorway frees souls from their bodies, and where, at the bottom of a well, dark secrets lie waiting to make things much, much worse. The collected first storyline of Hill's compelling new comics series mixes supernatural awe with page-turning dread.

Steampunk | BY AMANDA GANNON

A BESTIARY OF BRASS & BONE

Mad genius is how one wants to describe the impulse that's led Chicago artist Jessica Joslin to create a menagerie of beasts out of skulls and brass. And yet it's not megalomania, but a love of nature and a firsthand knowledge of animal anatomy that bring her creations to life.

Years' worth of scrounging junk shops, flea markets, hardware stores, and old attics has yielded a pack rat's horde of car parts and musical instruments, antique brassware and opera gloves. A wall of drawers in her studio contains fish scales, umbrella tips, glass eyes, universal ball joints, tiny bolts, miniature springs.

And then there are the skulls. Some are real bone, obtained from dealers in osteological specimens, and some are only replicas as clever as Joslin's creations themselves. She strives to make it impossible to tell which are real and which are not. In fact, the overall impression one gets from her animals, no matter how piecemeal or whimsical, is one of reality.

The assembly can take weeks, even months. In the depths of her studio, Joslin transforms the unlikely materials into creatures so plausible that one cannot imagine them reduced to their component parts. The almost Nouveau lines of their skeletal forms are lively, even when wrought of the most strange and inorganic of materials. A brass-boned dog in a leather harness raises one paw, his dark eyes eager to please, tail all but wagging. Caught in mid-swing, a monkey seems about to reach up to grab the next brass branch. The creatures always appear on the brink of motion.

On close examination, one realizes they *are*. Since welding would destroy the delicate patina on the antique parts, Joslin painstakingly joins them together with tiny bolts, springs, and couplings. The technique allows for all sorts of surprises: beaks open, tails flex, necks bend and jaws part. Some of Joslin's surprisingly sturdy beasts are freestanding and poseable. And like all animals, they are not always well-behaved: The artist has admitted that more than one of her creations has bitten her.

Yet these are clearly not mongrels spawned in a post-apocalyptic junk pile — these well-groomed creatures rest comfortably on upholstered cushions, wearing ruffs of silk and velvet. Their brass armatures are lovingly burnished, their white bones covered with filigree and ornamented with jewels and gewgaws. These are pampered luxury pets for the aristocrats of a world fashioned from the remnants of our own.

What began as a simple love for an ever-diminishing natural world has seemingly grown to encompass a parallel love of the discarded, a desire to use what has been left behind. There is a comparison to be made to taxidermy—but even the best taxidermy lacks the animation shown by these composite beasts, which don't in any way give the impression of being inanimate or dead. Joslin's creatures lack nothing; she has not preserved something vanished, but created something new: "I make my beasts because they are what I dreamed of discovering, but they didn't exist anywhere, so I had to make them myself."

Jessica's work can be viewed online at www.jessicajoslin.com, and her new book, *Strange Nature*, is now available from the Lisa Sette Gallery: www.lisasettegallery.com.

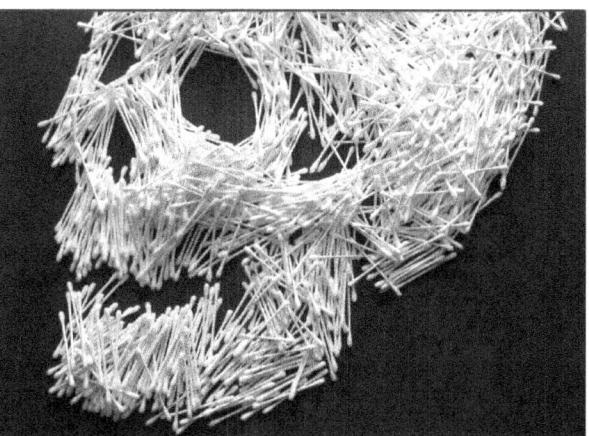

SKULL-A-DAY | *skulladay.blogspot.com*

The human skull is an instantly recognizable symbol, primal in appearance and visceral in impact: the hollows of the eyes and cheekbones, the empty hole of the nose, the grinning teeth. At once repellent and beautiful, it hits us where we live because we know, deep down, *that is our face*. Last year, internationally-known artist and activist Noah Scalin took the theme to heart and committed himself to creating a skull a day. Executed in an astonishing diversity of media including oil paint, sheet metal, food, and x-rays, the images are sometimes whimsical and often disturbing. The recently-completed project is chronicled online at Scalin's daily blog, where he also shares readers' found and created skull images. *Skulls*, a compilation of Scalin's Skull-A-Day work, will be released by Lark Books in October.

ART OF ADORNMENT | *artofadornment.ca*

Vancouver artist Elaine Foster, better known as Valerian, is the one-woman powerhouse behind Art of Adornment, an online store celebrating the Belle Époque fusion of style and beauty. Valerian has dedicated herself to providing quality, handmade items at a reasonable price. Using antique tools and the finest materials she creates chokers, hats, pins, watch chains and more. Collections such as Sanguine, Lucrezia, and Nocturne offer the browser a wide choice of colors and styles, and many of the handmade, one-of-a-kind items are customizable. Elegant, decadent, and darkly beautiful, Art of Adornment offers Victorian gothic accessories that are as unique as the wearer.

HARVEY PELICAN & CO., Favorite Unlikely Supply House on Earth, Ipswich.

DJINN DWELLING

Classical Element Compass № 1201

OFFERS MAGIC AT IMPOSSIBLE PRICES.

Aether Filter Home Unit № 1443

LIBERATED AT LAST? TRY OUR... GENIUS FOOTWEAR. page 165...

HARVEY'S WISH FOR YOU ON LABELING. Very intrusive, but necessary. The difference between 'bottle of spirits' and 'Spirits in bottles' is THE LABEL.

HUMAN EYE LENS Available in BLUE, GREEN, VACANT and BLOODSHOT.

The LUXAR TWO-STORY HOMESTEAD
◇◇◇◇◇◇◇◇◇◇
Furnishings & instruments untangible.

SMOKELESS FIRE PLACE. Flame available in: TRADITIONAL, PROPHETIC, TRANSMISSIBLE, TRANSPORTING and COLD.

BUDGET COMPLEX APARTMENT
◇◇◇◇◇◇◇◇◇◇
Phantom halls provide world class security.

MOVE IN TODAY

ASSORTED Animal VEILS

GOLDEN LION TAMARIN THERMAL.

NUMBAT CARDIGAN.

MALLARD CAPS.

COMPOSITION MARSUPIAL 85% RODENT 15%

MORTAL WEAR IS NORMAL. MILD SOAP. LINE DRY.

The Monster With the Shape of Me

BY BRIAN J. HATCHER

For a moment, I saw a rose die
just a little as I walked by.
The color of its petals waned,
the sun's benediction cruelly restrained,
by a monster with the shape of me.

But only a moment, and then I passed.
Then the bright crimson color, at last
returned, in an instant, freshly renewed,
the tender bud's hue no more subdued
by a monster with the shape of me.

Too often, I feel my gaze pulled down
to that black shape upon the ground
that gently kills but never buries,
for, in God's mercy, it seldom tarries,
that monster with the shape of me.

Yet, if I could but bear the sun
then I'd need never dwell upon
that form which mocks my every breath
and coldly tempts the earth with death,
that monster with the shape of me.

But the sun's bright face I cannot see.
It blinds, it burns, it accuses me.
Its fiery truth casts me away
into the arms of my decay.
A monster with the shape of me.

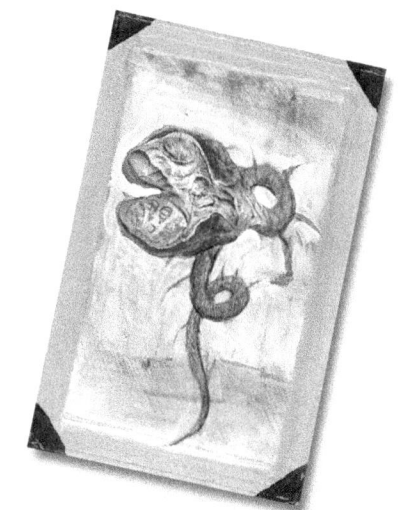

It hints to secrets in my past,
as if a smoky scrying glass
that knows my evils bound within.
It seems to me the soul of sin,
a monster with the shape of me.

And yet my terror is mine alone.
For this obsession is my own,
who sees the shadow on my wall
and fears the vapor that I call
the monster with the shape of me.

But soon, one day, my heart will still
as I am broken upon life's wheel.
And then, except perhaps a memory,
there will be nothing left to be
the monster with the shape of me.

ILLUSTRATION: "BLOOM" BY STEVEN ARCHER

VIKTOR KOEN

Our special guest cover artist chats with WEIRD TALES arts & culture editor **Amanda Gannon** about adaptation, transformation, and life at the center of the universe.

Businessmen are reborn as biomechanical insects. Beautiful and battle-ravaged woman/weapon hybrids haunt desolate landscapes. Such is the duality that infuses Viktor Koen's weird artwork.

Many of his figures are caught in the middle of some devastating transformation, or at the moment when the hidden becomes the apparent and the imagined becomes shockingly real. To Koen, everything contains a hidden nature, everything is constantly changing, and that's what makes his work so grimly fascinating—he sees this inner nature, and he shares his unflinching vision with us.

Born in Thessaloniki, Greece, Koen holds degrees from the Bezalel Academy of Arts & Design in Jerusalem and from the School of Visual Arts in New York City. He's a New Yorker, now, with an astounding litany of awards, exhibits, and high-profile clients.

His method underscores the transformative motif: his work itself has evolved from classical roots into a hybrid of digital and traditional forms, yielding images at once phantasmagorical and all too believable. It's not immediately apparent how much is real, how much artifice. The question is immaterial; it all must be taken at face value, for what Koen shows us is the very darkness hidden beneath the world's façade.

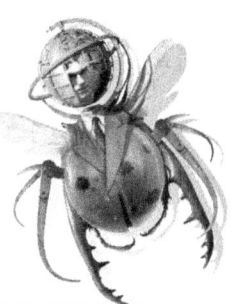

Your work is a complicated process, a synthesis of many methods. How do you pull together all of the elements? What are some of the stages an image goes through before it's complete?

Sometimes I do sketches, sometimes I don't. Sometimes I have something very specific in my mind from the first, and other times I let the image lead the way. As soon as I have the idea, I will compile my photographic references and the raw materials. I usually like to shoot details myself; I like to shoot interesting pieces of equipment, I shoot strange landscapes or sky formations when I see them.

Most times I shoot without really knowing when and how I will use the photographs, so in any specific project, half of the photographs I use are shots that I have already taken (for no other reason than my visual obsessions), and the other half are things that I specifically need to find and capture. This turns my job to a treasure hunt, but in this city there is one of everything and I will find it when I need it.

And then I start the painstaking process of cleaning things up. I do a lot of hand-tinting, and then assembling, and when I'm happy with the image and the composition, I start actually fusing the parts together. This fusion gets tricky since everything has been shot under different light conditions, so colors look different and light sources look different. I'm trying to homogenize all of these by hand tinting and lowering colors that are too vibrant so there's a color match between the pieces of the composition. And then, lighting: I like to use dramatic shadowing; that is a residue of projects I did on film noir covers quite a few years ago, and that was a turning point in the way I light and shade my images. I think the secret to a seamless composition is really balancing colors nd shadows.

You want your work to challenge people's assumptions. In exploring the themes of your work while you research and create it, have you ever found your own assumptions challenged?

Yes. A lot of information you get on the surface is very different from what you find out after in-depth research. I love to read, I love to research, I'm a history buff, so I will use the turns and twists according to the information I receive in the beginning, and try to incorporate things I learn. Especially in a series, by keeping things loose conceptually in the beginning, you give yourself some time to start putting the initial stages of the image together but also to read and find out if what you're doing is working, and to incorporate changes if need be. Concepts sometimes do change, evolve, take different turns.

Now if, in the process of one series, I run into something that is very different and unique, I might start a whole new series. I will use something from the research for a previous theme to start something totally new. I may run into something that is very exciting conceptually, and that always comes with the potential to create interesting images. It's sort of like a hydra, a monster . . . you cut one head and then two spring up, and I like that—I like to have an excuse to make more images.

What inspired you to move away from traditional media and into digital art?

I have to say that my transition from a person who painted in acrylics into a digital artist was a seamless one. I found that my projects work best with the realistic elements that photographs give you and paintings or drawings don't. So I like that twist, that momentary illusion or delusion of something looking real. I like making someone take a closer look, so that they discover the twist, delivered with the conceptual punch.

At first, I would compose things with photocopies, transfer them to sheets of acetate, and paint them with acrylics. Slowly the photocopying transformed into scan-

SKELEPHRON

ning, which was much cheaper than making countless photocopies of every single piece of reference. Also, gradually, by shooting more of my own references I used my sensibilities and sensitivities to create my inventory of raw materials. The painting turned into digital tinting and mixing of textures that I had photographed myself.

It took quite a few years to get from one to the other, but it happened gradually, until it came to a point where the process was totally digital but really deeply-rooted in traditional media. I don't think the technique I use is so advanced. I really consider myself very old-fashioned as far as digital art is concerned, but I like it this way.

My foundations are very traditional, very classical. I studied academic drawing and painting in Greece. A visual education doesn't get much more classical than this. I had to feel very stable in the foundations of what I do in order to grow and develop into a digital artist. Bringing everything I know

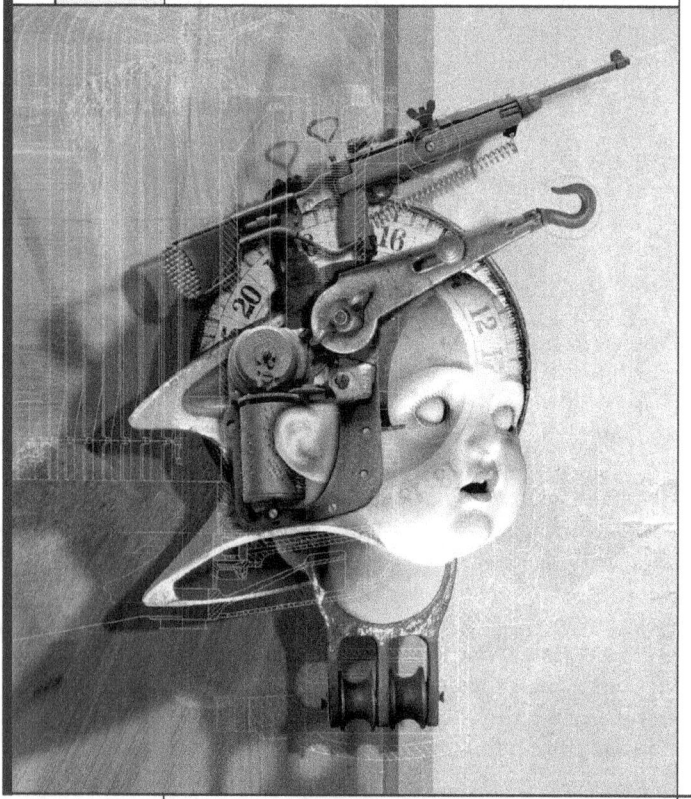

into one platform, the computer, was the only way for my images to work. That's what I like, pouring things onto the screen and experimenting with things that I scan or doodle or photograph or find. Then I can really do something with them. The computer becomes a great desktop—literally— to bring things together and fuse them, turn them into something totally different.

In your *Funnyfarm* series, there's a piece called "Future Shock," which is the idea that Western society is changing so rapidly that people are failing to change or adapt to meet new challenges. Now, you've clearly risen to meet the challenges of new technology— you're exploring that through your art. How do you think it's affecting the rest of the artistic world? Are you seeing future shock, or are you seeing evolution?

I don't believe people need to evolve if they don't want to. I mean, there's beautiful painting and drawing, there's a place for every kind of artwork. I think that people impose those limitations upon themselves and they panic, thinking they really need to be doing something new, all the time.

If you're good at what you're doing and you're passionate about it, I don't believe you have anything to worry about. In publishing and graphic design, you could not avoid the digital revolution. Even so, there are plenty of traditional print shops that produce beautiful work with hand-set and hand-cut type; they're using the traditional techniques of publishing. They are rare, sought-after and lucrative for the people who really have the drive to stick with what they love and want.

If you're someone who has things to say and is good at something, there's really no reason to move to [a style] that looks more advanced or fashionable or trendy. That's not the point. I think these future shocks are self-imposed. If you're always running after a belated "it," you will always be a victim of the latest "it."

Your subjects often combine the artificial with the actual. Your work is quite confrontational that way; it puts that duality right in your face. What is it that fascinates you so much about figures in transition or figures that aren't what they seem to be?

I love robots, I love anatomy. My father's an industrial designer, so I always loved drafting and calculations; I love the industrial design of all of this. I like the inner aspects of people, things, and animals. I wish I had x-ray glasses, in a way.

I guess it goes very well with the way I want to show the different, unpopular part of things, and that's where the conceptual strength of the imagery comes from. I think as soon as you turn any shell inside out, all the dirty laundry comes out. I think that everyone and everything is full of dirty laundry. That's not really visible to a lot of people, because a lot of people are not looking for it. A lot of people like to be appeased, a lot of people like hunky-dory, peaches and cream, and I'm exactly the opposite—I like piss and vinegar.

There's a lot of debate over the ultimate role of technology: whether it will ultimately lead to the best in us, or the worst. What do you think?

I don't think technology's evil; I think technology's what we make it. Humans were born to advance and push envelopes and limits, so we really have no choice. It comes down to individual responsibility. I believe in the power of one.

Technology is the tool to accomplish everything we need to accomplish and that's about it: accepting that we have to deal with it. I don't think there's use in debates over "is it good or bad?"—it is what it is. It just develops by the minute because we do. I think people should be debating what they will do with it, instead of thinking of it as good or bad. Unless you can afford to hide in the woods, you really have no choice but to be surrounded by technology.

DARK PECULIAR TOYS NO. 16

Technology is really up to you; should you allow your three-year-old to spend 24 hours in front of a TV set, or are you going to raise her? Will you let other people program her or will you make the effort to give her all you have, to help her learn, and take it from there? It's up to you to use a car or not, it's up to you how much electricity you're going to use or what kind of technology you're going to use, if you're going to be a victim of the media or if you are going to use it. Are you going to be a victim of the Internet, or are you going to *really* use it? The Web is such an amazing research tool in our hands, with unmatched ability to connect and educate. If you use it for gambling, it's a different story, and spending hours in front of a monitor is no way to go through life.

People who want to use technology for good will always find a way; people who would use it negatively will always find a way to abuse it, so it's really an individual choice. If people would realize that they can really make a difference in every single move they make, I think we would all be better off, but then I'm a firm believer that you vote with your pocketbook in everything you buy, and you make the best decisions you can.

Technology extends from us, it comes out of us, it is an extension of us, so it's really up to us.

What sort of assignments do you find most freeing? What excites you most?

I love coming up with solutions, so I'm very interested even in assignments that don't sound interesting on the surface, like financial publications. I'm having a lot of fun with some heavy-metal record packaging that I'm working on currently. I just finished some pieces for *Time* magazine

that were very challenging. So it's the subjects, and not the origins. Since I have a wide base of clients, the mix of projects is always different. I'm good at finding something that really interests me in each project; it might be something very technical, it might be something conceptual, it could be something compositional, or even the fact that I have so little time to do it—it's challenging to me.

I need to make every project mine and I need to be excited by every project, and it's very rare that I do something mechanically and finish it just because I have to. The boring technical things, clipping and feathering and mixing and matching, sometimes take a long time, so I do these things early in the morning when I have the most patience; then I do things involving thinking and conceptual development toward the end when I go to bed, right before sleep. That's when I look for riddles to solve.

Matching what I do to the time I do it has optimized my interest in both the work and my time management. It works for the best for me and my projects. This balance is very important to me, and it took years to accomplish. I also enjoy dealing with my clients, my book publishers and people from magazines and newspapers; I love the human contact, I love my discussions with them. I like brainstorming or troubleshooting over the phone or grabbing lunch and really exchanging ideas and touching base. I feel that I've been blessed with collaborations with top-notch professionals, and it's great working with them and learning from them.

It's a privilege that an illustrator is considered an artist and not a contractor, and that my opinion is valued and listened to. It's a collaborative endeavor that makes better pictures. Also, after working hours on end in a studio by yourself, it's great to get that contact with people, especially with great professionals, and make different kinds of friends.

You've traveled and exhibited all over the world, but you always come back to New York. What is it about New York that energizes you?

Everything about New York is energizing. Even though I come from far, far away, I consider myself a real New Yorker. If New York didn't exist, I'd have to create it. I love this place, I love the energy, I love the people that exude that energy, I love this amazing city that works very hard and produces the best. It's just such a big ongoing project, this city. I love being able to walk downstairs and find myself in the middle of the universe. Did I say I love this place?

I like the size of the city, but I have arranged my life in one extended neighborhood. I used to have a studio that was across the street from the stock exchange, but now I'm in the Gramercy area and I overlook the main School of Visual Arts building across the street, so it's a really nice neighborhood. My studio is upstairs from home. Both universities I teach in, Parsons and the School of Visual Arts, are within eight or ten blocks, so I go everywhere on foot.

It's a place I could endlessly walk around and explore; New York is filled with things that make me feel like a tourist as soon as I discover them. I can hardly believe I live here. I love this excitement, this feeling that you're really part of something, of being open to surprises. There's something every day that makes me think, "Only in New York City."

It's great to live in a place that is so many people's destination, and it's great to go away and miss it and come back. It's such a great place to call home.

What are you working on now? What's your next project?

I had a book signing at the New York Comic-Con this year. The event was coordinated with Baby Tattoo Books, a small publishing house from the West Coast that impressed me with their catalogue. I was

MUTUCUS

also impressed with the publisher, Bob Self, who I met at last year's BookExpo America. We're working on a book based on my *Dark Peculiar Toys* series, and it's scheduled to be presented at the *next* New York Comic-Con! A good relationship with a publisher is paramount for an artist with a sweet tooth for books, and I am looking forward to the next one.

Other than that, this year has been heavy in participations to group shows around the world, from Athens to Little Rock to Beijing, and a few symposium lectures. But the day-to-day activities revolve around book and magazine covers so please be careful in book stores! You never know when my images will ask you to do some thinking. ℮

✳ **See more artwork:**
www.viktorkoen.com

First Photograph

BY ZORAN ŽIVKOVIĆ

ILLUSTRATED BY SCOTT MAXWELL | TRANSLATED FROM THE SERBIAN BY ALICE COPPLE-TOŠIĆ

Appearances can be deceiving. You look at a picture and think you see everything. Young mother with babe in arms. Indeed, what else is there to see? You've seen thousands of such photographs. Even on postcards. It's a cliché, you think.

And yet it isn't. Take a closer look. The two-month-old child (me, although, of course, you can't recognize me on my first photograph) seems intent on holding its head where it's not supposed to be, under its mother's bosom, closer to her stomach.

There's something unnatural about that position. One would expect the baby to long to hear its mother's heartbeat. That's why mothers instinctively hold babies with their head cradled in their left arm.

I suppose I too (although, to tell the truth, I don't remember) loved to hear my mother's throbbing heart. How could it be otherwise? I was a normal baby.

Or perhaps not quite normal. I knew something that, even if I could, I wouldn't have told anyone. Because it wasn't normal. At least not according to the standards of the time. Today people would probably have a different take on it all. Be more indulgent. At least I hope so.

Here, let's check it out. I'll tell you the secret why I, this weak little baby, was trying with might and main to listen beneath my mother's bosom. I wanted so terribly to hear the beating of another heart that was down there a bit lower.

No, my mother didn't have two hearts. Not at all. Anatomically and in all other respects, everything about her was in perfect order. She certainly would have been horrified to learn about that other heart, particularly since it wasn't hers and yet was located inside her.

Well, all right, whose other heart could that be, you wonder with a certain understandable surprise, in the normal mother of a two-month-old baby?

Here's the answer. The other heart beating in my mother's body belonged to my twin brother. I would like to call him by name, but he was never given one. Not only because he was never born. Had my parents known that he was conceived when I was, they would certainly have had a name waiting for him. As they did for me. But there was no ultrasound at the time.

Wait, wait, I can already hear your interruptions, what do mean to say—he wasn't born? How could he still not be born two months after your birth? All-embracing medicine has yet to record such an event. Without mentioning the fact that your mother, even after bringing you into the world would have been—and looked, which is more important—pregnant.

It truly would have been like that, and your amazement quite fitting, had things taken their natural course. But they didn't. Exactly two months and eleven days after my twin brother and I were conceived, he decided not to be born. It's true we were only fetuses at the time, but you are terribly mistaken if you think such far-reaching decisions can't be made so early on.

All right, not all fetuses are equally mature. Take me, for example. Something like that would never have crossed my mind. I was much more ingenuous. Nothing more

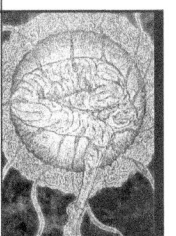

far-reaching than enjoying the warm, safe surroundings of my mother's womb interested me. But even then my brother was characterized by a seriousness and responsibility of which few can be proud, among newborns and adults alike.

His decision astonished me, of course. How else could it be? I had counted on us being born together as befits identical twins. How could I enter the world by myself, deprived of the closest relative imaginable? It's not certain I could even consider myself a twin in that case.

Completely distraught, I asked for an explanation. But I didn't get one. All I was told, in the special nonverbal way that fetuses communicate, is that that's the way it had to be. As though Fate itself were talking. It was not until much later that I realized it actually could not have been otherwise. The explanation went far beyond my capacity to understand at that age. It's questionable that I could even today. I sincerely doubt that I will ever reach an understanding of the world to match that of my brother when he was just a fetus.

While I was unable to grasp his reasons for not being born, I wanted to know how he intended to pull it off. This was a technical, not metaphysical question, so I hoped that I would be able to understand it. Was he intending to keep growing and developing in Mother's stomach until he came of age, and even afterward? I was horrified at the thought of what our mother would look like with a grown man in her stomach.

He took me soundly to task for such a vicious thought. Of course he wouldn't keep on growing. How could he spoil his own mother's appearance? He wouldn't even stay in his current tiny proportions that would certainly cause her no inconvenience. He would go to the opposite extreme. Become smaller.

I must have given him a dumbfounded look with my large fetus eyes, because he hastened to dispel my doubts. Why was I so surprised? We live in an age of miniaturization, don't we? Everything's getting smaller

and smaller. We're coming closer to a quantum world in all respects. It turns out that even the cosmos itself isn't quite as enormous as was once thought. So why should fetuses be any exception?

What else could I do but accept this rational explanation. But this did nothing to lessen my concern. When do you intend to start shrinking, I asked him. Sensing fear in my inaudible voice at the possibility of being all alone, he firmly promised that nothing would happen before I was born. He would maintain his current size until then.

And indeed, while I continued to grow, he didn't change. Over time I became so large compared to him that I had to be very careful not to accidentally harm him. Moving about like every lively baby at the end of its term in the womb, I could have smothered him, pressed him or even smashed him.

My anxiety grew as the delivery date approached. It's a tumultuous event, something could go wrong. What if he didn't manage to stay inside? If he came out with me, he wouldn't even be a premature baby. The obstetrician and midwife might not even notice him.

He just waved his bud of a hand dismissively at my anxious questions. I was not to worry, everything was taken care of. He was always to the point when important matters were involved.

He was able to console me in that regard, but not about our parting. It was clear to me that Fate was behind the whole thing, but this didn't make it any easier for me. Is there anything harder than taking leave of your twin brother? It's like parting with your own self. But we're not parting, he assured me. I won't die, I'll just get smaller. And I won't go anywhere. You'll be able to hear my heart whenever you put your ear to Mother's stomach.

Just as he promised, the delivery went smoothly. For both of us. And for Mother too. In spite of her exhaustion, she was cheerful, and everyone misunderstood my cries. They shouldn't be criticized for this, though. Every

Zoran Živković is a writer, essayist, researcher, editor, publisher and translator from Belgrade, Serbia, where he still resides. He is the author of seventeen works of fiction including *The Fourth Circle* (1993), *Time Gifts* (1997), *The Last Book* (2007) and *Escher's Loops* (2008). Živković has been nominated for several awards and received the Miloš Crnjanski Award, World Fantasy Award, the Isidora Sekulić Award, and the Stefan Mitrov Ljubiša Award for Life Achievement in Literature. His work has been translated into more than twenty languages.

baby cries at birth. How could they suppose that my tears were from parting with a brother no one knew about?

Although quite weak, ever since Mother first drew me to her breast I made every effort to put my little head on her stomach. At first she found it unusual and brought my head back up, but she got used to it over time. Particularly since I fell asleep the fastest in that position. And what mother wants to have trouble putting her baby to sleep?

My brother's heartbeats, although barely audible, had a calming effect on me. We were no longer touching like before, but we were separated by the very small partition of Mother's skin and a thin layer of fat. You could even say that we were still connected. Just like when we were happily inhabiting the same body.

Well, no idyll is ever of long duration. This one ended when I was four and a half months old. Not all at once, but over three days. At first I thought there was something wrong with my hearing. I had to press my head harder and harder into Mother's soft abdomen to make out the sound of the tiny heart inside.

And then with horror I realized the truth. My brother had set out on the final minimization. At the end of the third day I could no longer hear him regardless of my efforts. And I couldn't try any harder because Mother's stomach had started to hurt from all my pressing, so she held me away from it.

Inevitably I fell ill. Many adults, let alone a baby, would have been crushed by such a trauma. My illness caused the doctors great concern. No one could discover its cause. They examined me thoroughly and tried various therapies, but nothing helped improve my blood count and bring back my appetite. And pull me out of my apathy.

I got better at the beginning of my sixth month. They thought it happened all by itself. The doctors couldn't find the reason for

this spontaneous recovery either. But it caused them no concern. Who cares why things are going fine, while they are? They didn't miss a chance, however, to give themselves credit for this favorable turn of events.

And the credit was all mine. I simply started to look at things rationally. At that age a lot of maturing happens in a month and a half, even when you're sick. Or rather, particularly then.

All right, I can't hear my brother's heart anymore, but that doesn't mean, as he himself said, that he died. He's still alive in Mother's womb, he just got smaller. To the quantum level. Maybe even below it. Indeed, miniaturization truly knows not boundaries. And there, as we all know, it's completely immaterial to talk about sound, so there isn't any beating.

This silence from the womb actually came at just the right time. I couldn't keep my head on Mother's stomach forever. What would that look like? Babies have to be weaned sooner or later. It's a bit hard in the beginning, but then they get used to solid food. And start enjoying it.

I rarely think of my brother today. You know how it is: out of sight, out of mind. I only remember him when I look at this photograph, and I don't do that very often. You can't see him, but I know he's there. And I hope he's well wherever he is now. In any case, it was his own choice.

I don't know whether I've convinced you, though. I'd say I haven't. Congratulations on the quantum world, I can almost hear you thinking, but if a person doesn't believe their own eyes, whom will they believe and why? Appearances can be deceiving, but not that much. The picture only shows an ordinary young mother with babe in arms. And since the baby truly doesn't look like me now at this advanced age, how can you believe me when I say it's me? Particularly since my penchant for wild ideas earned me a bad reputation long ago. I'm even trying to make a living out of it. ☙

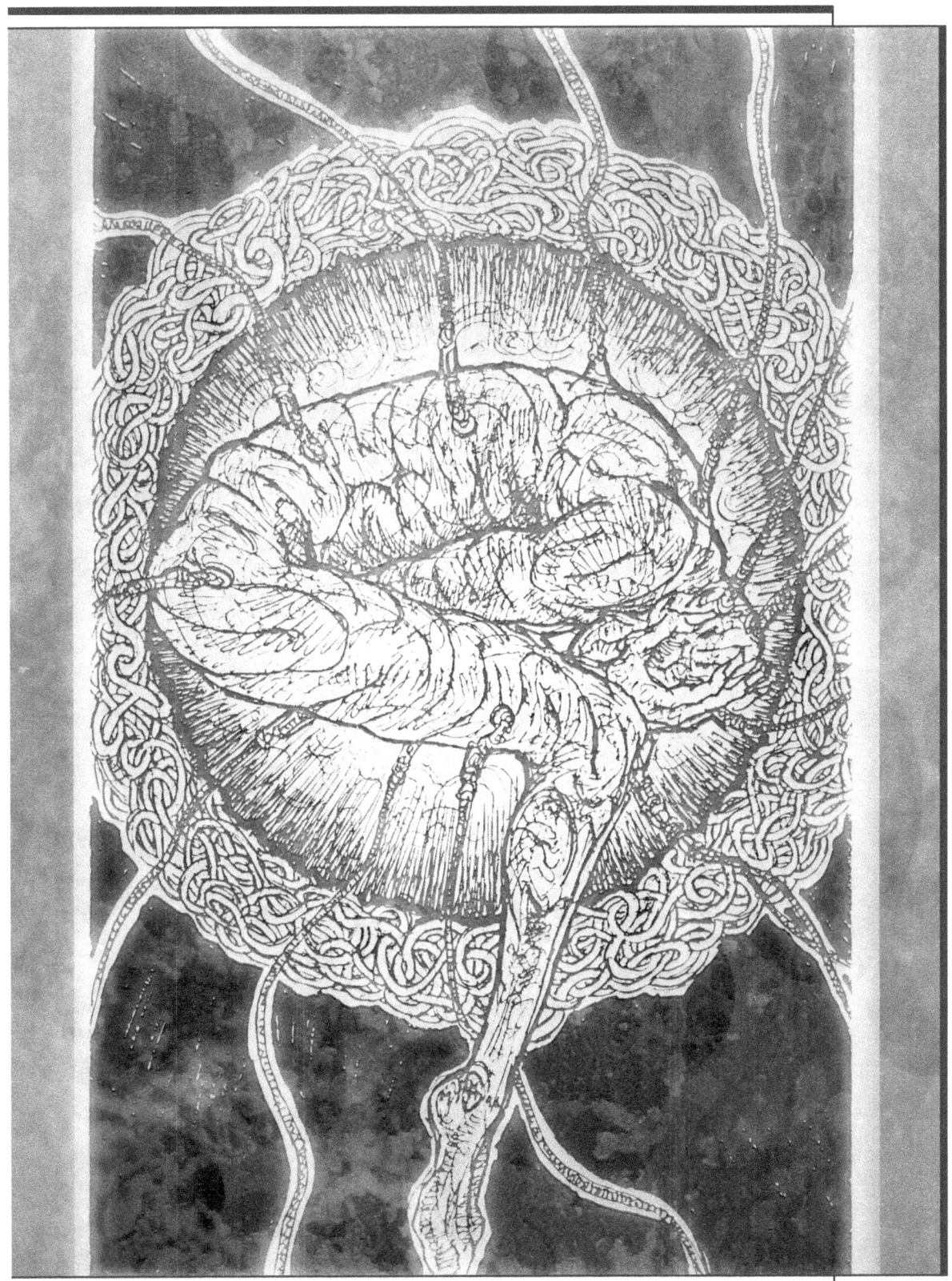

The Gong

BY SARA GENGE

ILLUSTRATION BY JOY PRESCOTT

IN WHICH THE
SWORD BATTLE
IS VICIOUS & AN
UNMAN'S SCHEME
IS MORE SO

O N THE EVE of the battle, the Gong chimed from the turret on the temple. The sound vibrated through the metal fittings on the city's walls and onto the warriors armour, making nobling spears and peasant hoes quiver alike.

If you were touching the ground that day you must have felt it, rising from your bare feet, up your thin, fat, agile or decrepit legs, through your loins (may you always keep them) and on to your stomach, your heart, maybe your vocal cords. If you opened your mouth at that moment you may have exhaled a perceptible—ahhh—a reflex sound, a sigh of death and probable defeat.

In my case, the vibration stopped at my loins, or what was left of them. I do not think it was because of an obsession with that missing part of my anatomy but that the missing link stopped the chain reaction, my body could relay the sound no further and it died there, with my unborn children and my weakness.

The peasants took it well, they collected their miserable belongings, their families and their animals and moved in a steady flow towards the citadel. How it must have shone for them, the tungsten walls, ornate decorations, white drapes on slender windows! Even then, nimble archers peered out from them, noting landmarks that would help them aim later on.

The better informed warriors trembled. Some buried their gold, although we knew that if the Farong came that would be our last concern. Some polished old armour and set for the castle, but those were too few. Most ran, or hid in stubborn glue bunkers hoping the enemy would overlook them.

Only Aghar kept his cool and ordered us to form, trembling halfmen, under the white battle flags of the turret. In those days he was cold as a knife and the wind whipped his hair against his copper jaw. His words were crisp and surgical, cutting into our bowels and releasing us from our fear. We, the eunuchs, would fight the Farong! Alone if we must.

We were poorly trained, of course, but not as desperate as the peasants that even now were being recruited to defend the city. We were all noble-born, although our families had fallen in disgrace, and had all received standard battle training before we were put to the knife. I fumbled with my sword and dagger, trying to remember the knowledge that I had so easily wielded when I was twelve and wincing at the easy muscularity of the whole men around me.

Rumours said that the nobles were refusing to fight, holding back, they said, as shock troops for the day when the need was dire. I knew they were stalling, pulling strings, making alliances and even sending parleys among the dreaded Farong to see when to throw their weight, and with whom.

We marched to see the King, Aghar speaking for us all. The Law says a eunuch cannot fight, but His Majesty sighed and laid a two fingered benediction on Aghar's nehilim sword. After that, nobody tried to stop us.

When the Farong came, we left the citadel and went out to the trampled dirtbowl to meet them. Their first instinct was to jeer at us. I can still hear their battle cries, their coy seductions and their threats. The Farong women stood out like jewels on the field, diamond tipped spears and well oiled scales reflecting the light like myriad green prisms. Their partners marched by their female's sides, five men to each wife.

Aghar surveyed the scene calmly, as if we weren't staring at our deaths. When they cut him, they took away from his skin the capacity to wrinkle, and his face seemed flat and inscrutable, like that of a young girl who does not wish to be married. His hair, which had been oiled by kings in the bedchamber, now flew loose in the wind.

Aghar barked his orders.

We spread out and formed three columns, the better trained Sworn Maidens on the sides, eunuchs and conscripts in the centre. Farong fight in family packs with their females as leaders. Discipline is exquisite inside each pack and every male has a rank which is achieved through a complex scale of feats, but they don't have an overall strategy of war. Still, they outnumbered us five to one.

We did what we could, but soon the central column started to fold. Eunuchs are trained for the bedchamber, not for the sword. Aghar's orders kept us fighting but we were ceding ground. The enraged Farong inched in on us.

"Central column, retreat!"

I ran for my life.

The enemy came after us and was surrounded by the Sworn Maidens. I scrambled into their left column and they let me pass to safety with amused grins.

Shrieks pierced the air. In my flight, I slipped on red and green blood. Soon there were no more formations and I did not know where to run. My companions were scattered and Aghar had his hands full, directing the Sworn Maidens to where they could do the most harm.

I stood trembling, the sun beating down on my helmet. I could not run much further. Around me, green Farong limbs continued to twitch, even after being severed from their bodies.

At first it seemed the Maidens had the situation under control, but I soon realized that many felled Farong were regenerating and getting up to join the battle again.

Without hesitation I walked to the nearest fallen brute and severed her head. I stood next to her, watching, but she stayed down. The other eunuchs picked up the idea. Soon, we were joined by the conscripts and by some of the wounded Maidens.

It took a while, but when the Farong saw there was no hope for them once they'd fallen, they retreated.

There is nothing so enticing as a running enemy. The blood frenzy went to my head and I started to fight in earnest, without care for my safety, swinging my sword wildly, parrying, attacking, cutting, crushing and maiming what stood in my way. After a while, somebody pulled me back and dragged me to camp.

That's all I remember of the first day.

THAT NIGHT, I oiled Aghar's back until he seemed to melt under my hands and asked him what he thought of our chances.

"It won't be so easy tomorrow, they will have learned from this mistake," he whispered. I trembled, my shoulders ached from supernatural fatigue and I didn't know if I could fight again.

"If the nobles don't commit themselves…" he sighed.

"The Sworn Maidens are the best…" I muttered, trying to appease him. It hurt me to see him worried.

"But there are just too few of them!"

I winced. I'd been trained to please and I took a man's anger as a personal rebuke. Aghar noticed.

"Poor Telora, come here," he said, holding my head against his chest. "Don't worry, the nobles will come and all will be well."

* * *

THE NEXT DAY, Aghar placed most of the eunuchs on top of a small hill and let the Sworn Maidens and the conscripts form to our right. Then he walked among the ranks of Sworn Maidens and chose one of every three to join us. This way, the enemy would see roughly an equal number of men and women on each flank. Farong are bad at distinguishing men from eunuchs, especially in armour.

When the Gong chimed, the Maidens attacked the Farong. When the beasts turned towards us, they found we had the upper ground and they struggled to push us back. They hissed among themselves and turned back towards the Maidens, but then we attacked, downhill, easily and crushed them between us.

AGHAR WAS NOT satisfied.

"They're only playing with us. It's mating season and they're itching to prove themselves. Once they've settled down for the year they will come at us in earnest and little clockwise tactics aren't going to do the trick."

I muttered abjectly, desperate to cheer him up. I was brought up to believe that my main function was to make my masters happy, and although Aghar was more a friend than a master, it still bothered me to see him like this. Battle hadn't changed me that much. I was in awe of the spasm that took hold of me in the battlefield and incited me to kill without remorse or regard of consequence, but once the battle was over I was back to my diffident self. I wondered if that was not the fundamental difference between men and people such as me: both men and eunuchs can be aroused to sex or bluster, but while eunuchs forget violence and sex when the occasion passes, men hold those two things dear in their minds and let them guide all their actions during their waking hours.

"It would take the Sworn Maidens' drug to win this war, Telora, and the Gods know there's no way the Sworn will give us their magic."

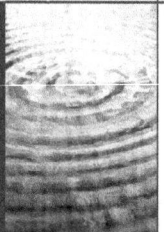

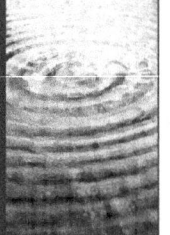

"There must be some way," I muttered.

He smiled. "Don't be afraid, Telora. I have made my peace with this war and the death that it'll surely bring me. I need you to promise me one thing. When I'm sure I cannot hold them any longer, I'll give you this sign." He gestured with his hand. "I'll send someone trustworthy to bring it to you. When you see it, leave the city and don't stop until you've crossed the Riatsu River. Don't look behind, because I won't be following you."

"What? Desert? Never!"

He swung his head and smiled dryly, and I admired how his hair moved against his cheeks and shone in the lamplight, full as a woman's. One of the advantages of the surgery is that we never go bald.

"Do you love me, Telora," he said.

I could only nod.

"Then you will do as I say. I will defend my city to the last, if you promise to run when I tell you to. I can suffer to see you risk your life in battle, but I need to know you have a chance to survive."

I promised. It was the first lie I had ever told him and I hoped it would be the last.

DAYS PASSED AND we managed to keep the Farong at bay. Barely.

I fought next to the Sworn Maidens each morning, marvelling at their near invincibility and at the respect they managed to gleam even from the Farong. The huge reptiles had learned their lesson and studiously avoided crossing swords with the Sworn in the battlefield whenever they could.

Each day, my sword felt heavier, and the morale of our ragged army fell just a bit more. Only the Sworn kept up their chants. If they lost this war, they would simply move to the next citadel and offer their swords to a different King.

Then, the morning came when fear caught up with me and I could go on no longer. I stood with my squadron, waiting to go into battle and fought to keep my lungs from bursting. I had known fear before and

I had seen death before, but the panic which gripped me for no good reason was stronger than anything I'd ever encountered. It possessed me in a way I hadn't thought was possible. It left me empty of logic or conscience. By the time the panic retreated, I had arrived at a conclusion. I would not stand and let the fear take me again. I would not be passive. I would find a way to win this war, once and for all.

I went to battle absent-mindedly and if the Gods had willed it, I would have died many times that day.

Sneaking into the Sworn Maidens' camp wouldn't be easy. They were protective of the drug that made them stronger than any male and didn't like strangers wandering around. Considering what I was planning on doing, theirs was a reasonable concern.

The camp was well guarded and I was no match for the Sworn's legendary strength. No, stealing the drug wasn't even a possibility. If I was going to get it and make the eunuchs and the conscripts strong enough to win the war, I had to be subtle. I had been called beautiful in the past, and always by men, but I'd felt the Sworn Maidens' stares and I had enough experience to recognize the look. They were rough women of war and didn't realize they were so obvious, but I knew all the games.

The next couple of days, I polished my armour and wore my jewellery strategically, the best to enhance my lips, my arms and legs, and draw their eyes to me.

Finally, I was confident that anyone who wished to notice me had noticed me in the battlefield. I still needed to find a Maiden, so I set out that night and pressed into the darkness until I found a hiding spot in the bushes next to the Sworn's camp.

From my hiding spot, I searched for a candidate. The guard was talkative and open, but she was too old, and Sworn Maidens aren't stupid. If I made a pass, she'd know something was amiss. No, I needed someone younger, someone who would genuinely believe that, contrary to nurture and surgery, I might be interested in her.

I waited. The women went to bed, but I decided to stay and watch the change of guards. It would be useful to know their patterns. If my plan succeeded, I would have to creep into the camp often to join my lover in her tent.

The moon inched through the sky as I lay in the damp grass. After a couple hours, my shoulders stopped twitching with excitement and I dozed, but that was not a problem. I was no soldier, and I knew it. As long as I awoke every time the guard changed, I had all the information I needed. I had been trained to awake at the slightest sound when I was prepared to serve the bed of the King.

Dew chilled me to the bone, but still I waited. Dawn rose with a peach coloured cheek and showed me my bride. She was almost a girl, maybe sixteen, and although the Sworn Maidens' drug had made her more muscular than any man, she still had a tenderness to her skin and a shine to her eye that spoke of innocence and a soft heart.

I felt a pang of guilt for what I was about to do and allowed myself to feel remorse for a few seconds. Then I pushed my feelings into a corner, as I'd been trained to do, and slowly retreated away from the camp. I had a couple hours left to sleep, and I would need time to bathe, oil and paint my face before I met this girl in battle.

I WHISPERED MY request to Aghar and he placed me in the same column as the girl. I couldn't tell if he realized what I was up to, but I suspect that even if he had known, he wouldn't have interfered. If there was any way to win the war, it was my way.

I fought myself into her chisel group and engaged a Farong female who surpassed me in ability and strength. My Maiden gasped as I fought with the green creature, clearly amazed that such a delicate being as me would dare stand up to the brute. Predictably, the Farong disarmed me, and I fell on the ground, holding up my

light shield as only protection.

The enemy waited until her husbands gathered before closing in for the kill. It was the mating season after all, and only her valour guaranteed that her mates would stay with her one more year.

"So, little man," the Farong hissed. "You thought you could kill me?" I knew she wasn't taunting me; Farongs don't understand sarcasm. She was genuinely curious as to whether I had thought I could beat her in battle.

"A man's luck is his own," I said, using the time to crawl back towards the Sworn Maidens. I was frantic. I didn't know if the girl had noticed me. *Damn you, Telora!* How pathetic to die trying to attract a woman's attention.

The males around her scratched their scales with their claws making a noise like metal on stone. The female threw her head back, aroused by the sound, and I knew I was dead.

"Wait!" The girl jumped out from her formation.

"Come back here, Lea! He's not our problem," an older woman shouted.

"I won't let him die. He's been brave. Courage should be. . . rewarded," she said, flitting her eyes in my direction and holding her spear in front of her.

"Very well," the Farong said. "I'll kill you first."

From my position in the dirt, I watched the combat unfold. The males stood back, letting the female Farong prove her valour. My girl wasn't scared. Her spear didn't tremble. She circled around the Farong carefully, countering and paring, gauging her enemy's strength. I knew the real combat hadn't started yet; both dames were testing each other's strengths rather than attacking in earnest.

The fighters around them respected the duel and kept on with their private combats. It was infantry at its best, woman against woman, with honour. The dream of any warrior Maiden.

The Farong was at her prime, probably in her third decade, full of eggs that needed fathers and everything to gain from risking her life in the battlefield. I wondered if I had made a mistake by choosing her for my half-baked girl.

I shouldn't have worried. My girl had a trick up her sleeve. She lunged to keep the Farong occupied, unsheathed a stiletto and threw it at her enemy. The Farong fell back, twitching, nehilim knife wedged firmly into her eye socket.

I jumped up and decapitated her before she could regenerate.

"Hey! She was mine, you half-man!" the girl shouted. The Sworn Maiden have customs regarding the bodies of their dead enemies. Every evening, they insisted on collecting the bodies and carrying them off to their camp.

"Of course, my lady. I meant to save you this gory business," I said, as if she weren't already covered with blood and guts from a dozen kills. "A beauty like you shouldn't have to bother with this." I pointed at the decapitated body and showed my disgust. "You are much too valuable as a killer. Once a Farong goes down, some lesser soldier should handle the beheading for you."

She preened. "You could be right. Get behind me, and I'll give you all the beheadings you've ever dreamed of."

I followed her around, pretending to be enthused by the gore, but it paid off because that night she allowed me into her tent and let me wash the blood off her body. Then she sent me away, which was predictable. Sworn Maidens are virgins—in theory. But it was one thing to betray her vow and another to do so in the open with a man she'd just met.

That night, she crept into my tent in the eunuch's camp. I have no idea how she knew where I was sleeping, but I guess Sworn tracking skills were to blame. I gave myself over to her as best I could, and tried to imagine Aghar in my arms instead of this pale scarred woman.

* * *

All institutions die in the end, and the Sworn Maidens' virginity wasn't an exception. The other women accepted that Lea took me as a pet, and I was only too glad not to have to creep through the guards to get to my lover.

Lea started behaving like I was part of her army, and even shot herself the drug in front of me. I stared longingly at the vials, hoping she'd relent and offer me some. If I could take it back to my camp, Aghar would find a way to replicate it. She didn't volunteer any information and we settled into a routine where we fought by day and loved by night.

"TO EVERY WEAPON," the old Maiden said, holding her crotch and looking around to build suspense, "there is a counter-weapon!" she laughed, pointing at me. Lea giggled under the influence of the potato alcohol I'd brought with me to the Sworn's camp. The women gathered around and drank, their tongues growing looser throughout the night. There was a temporary truce while the Farong mated and Aghar got supplies from the country side, so we were fairly certain we'd be able to sleep in late the next morning.

I patted Lea's leg. It was now or never. If I couldn't extract the secret from her tonight, I might as well give up all hope.

"There's a balance in all things," Lea nodded wisely. The other women settled down into a more philosophical vein, spouting bits of wisdom that only seemed important because they were drunk.

I played along.

"The wise say that there are three sides to each entity," I had forgotten most of my philosophy, but I knew none of the women were sophisticated enough to catch me if I made a mistake. "Man, woman, eunuch. Animal, vegetable, symbiont. Land, sky, horizon . . ."

"Farong, noble, Maiden," Thera whispered.

"But each contains the seed of the other. A woman with too much is a man, a man with too little is an eunuch," I said.

The women murmured sympathetically.

"I'd give anything to be as strong as you are and as worthy of defending my city," I sighed and caught Lea's eye.

"What can't be, can't be," the older women murmured, but Lea held my hand until they were gone, and then took me to her tent.

"To everything, there is a balance, and a life-force in all creatures," she recited, as she shot me a vial of the Maidens' drug. "To fight the Farong, you must become the Farong, take them into you and be one with your enemy." I looked into her eyes and suddenly understood that the Sworn Maidens' drug was made from the enemy corpses they were so careful to claim after battle.

I had what I wanted, but still I stayed and loved her one more night, and then sprinted into the dew, my legs bouncing effortlessly off the wet ground.

I WAS AWAKE for hours before the Gong chimed. Now I understood the Maidens' endless energy. My camp woke around me and I grew more and more furious as I watched them stretch out stiff limbs and gather body armour with exasperating sloth. I had fought side by side with these men for weeks, but today I hated them. They were like restraints, keeping me away from battle. When they were ready, there was even more waiting before they formed and started marching towards the battleground.

The Sworn were already there and greeted us with hoots and contemptuous looks. At other times their rudeness had offended me, but now I understood that they were sick of waiting for a ram-shack army that couldn't get its act together. They were aching for the fight as much as I was, and my sword trembled in my hand from pent up energy.

When the Gong sounded for the second time, I jumped into battle with a feeling of relief. Luck was on my side: arrows missed me by hair-widths when I swayed slightly to avoid them, blows only fell on my shield,

where the friction stopped the enemy sword just long enough for me to counter-attack. I stayed by Aghar's side, elated to be able to protect him and anxious to show him my power.

"WHAT HAVE YOU done?" Aghar whispered when the battle was over. I raised an eyebrow and he sighed and lay back on the pillows.

"The Sworn Maidens' drug," he muttered, answering his own question. "It was a brash thing to do, Telora, it could hurt you. No man has ever tried it before."

"Well, I'm not exactly a man, am I?" I smiled and crept up to muzzle his chest. His smell filled me with love. I stopped when I saw Aghar's face. He looked like he was carrying a terrible burden, and his sadness killed whatever mood had filled the tent.

"I have betrayed her, I suppose," I whispered. That thought had pierced my drugged mind a dozen times throughout the day. I had done it for a reason and I would do it again, but I couldn't help but think of the pain I would cause Lea.

"Yes, I suppose," Aghar said.

I sat back, stunned. I had expected love and forgiveness but Aghar wasn't being spiteful, only stating facts. If he had shouted at me, or even been jealous of my little liaison, I could have attributed his words to anger or fear for my safety. But he lay back calmly on his rugs and stared at me as if he were trying to see through my eyes and into my brain.

"Find out how they make this drug." He waved in my direction. "I'll put someone to work on reproducing it, but I won't give it to anyone until we see what it does to you. Try to get the Sworn girl to give you more: I can't risk my army until I know it's safe. A fortnight's test should do the trick."

He didn't say it, but I knew I was dismissed. Aghar was too good a commander to reject a good tactic, but although he would use treason to win the war, he wouldn't tolerate the traitor in his bed. We were fin-

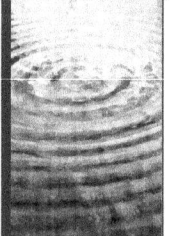

ished. I was surprised at how numb I felt.

I crawled back to my own tent, knowing that I was too distraught and exhausted to go back to my Maiden that night. I curled up in my pelts and tried to cry but the drug wouldn't allow me even that solace. My sadness sunk to the bottom of my gut, never again to surface. I tried to hate myself but I was too tired even for that. I felt the energetic effect of the drug fading and I realized that the difficult part of being a Sworn Maiden wasn't fighting, it was staying awake to party afterwards. That's why they valued party goers so much. It took training and self-control to stay alert after the drug wore off.

TWO WEEKS LATER, Aghar decided the drug was safe, but I hadn't been able to discover how they made it. Lea shared with me regularly, but I'm not sure even she knew how Farong bodies had to be processed to extract the strengthening components.

The last couple of days we sustained heavy loses. If we were going to win the war, we had to do it now. In those last days I kept looking for Aghar in the battlefield and making excuses to go near his tent in the evening. I tried to be subtle interrogating his helpers, his lovers, but by now the whole camp knew that I had fallen out of Aghar's grace.

I wonder; if I had known what was about to happen, would I have been capable of preventing it? Sometimes, I wake in the dead of night, sweating. I sit up in bed and feel the darkness press in on me, the erratic breath of alien bodies and the musk which surrounds me wherever I go. At those times, what frightens me the most is not whether I could have stopped that madness, but weather I would have tried to stop it if I had known. Would I have done what was right, or would I have bowed my head to the inevitable as I'd done countless times before?

The strategy for that last battle was particularly complex. Whenever I caught a glimpse of him, Aghar carried a furrowed

brow and spoke in urgent tones to his counsellors. I saw a runner come and go from the citadel, probably to seek council from the King. I guess it was one last attempt on Aghar's part to bring the nobles to our side.

I didn't understand the formation, but that wasn't new. I was placed in the centre of a circle with the Sworn Maidens, surrounded on three sides by eunuchs and conscripts whose numbers directed the enemy towards our central chisel.

Aghar waited until the battle was well under way before launching his plan. He had hand-picked a few dozen men, chosen from different units so that they wouldn't be missed. These men stayed back, and when the Maidens were deep in battle, they raided their camp. The girls on guard were dispatched with difficulty, but even the Sworn can't hold out five to a one. Still, one of them managed to sound the alarm. The Maidens realized what was going on and tried to get back to their camp, but they were surrounded by enemy on one side and by traitors on the others. No matter how much they pleaded, the men wouldn't let them out of the formation.

Even betrayed, the Sworn didn't become traitors, and wouldn't kill their allies even to save themselves. They had to cut through the Farong to get out of that battle, and by the time they made their way to camp, their potion had been stolen and there were five hundred superhuman men charging at the Farong.

In one day, they used the monthly allowance for the whole Sworn camp. They crushed the Farong and forced them to retreat to the other side of the city. Back in their camp, for the first time since anyone could recall, Sworn Maidens were seen crying.

The citadels walls opened and even the noblings came out to congratulate us on our success.

The Maidens wouldn't enter the city. They sent Lea as an emissary and stayed in their camp.

"What have you done?" she whispered once we were inside, pressing her stiletto under my belt. I bowed my head, and she seemed to remember my defect, because she poised the stiletto on my stomach instead.

"We were going to lose!" I said.

"So what?"

I stared at her in disbelief. Her face softened and she ran her hand through my hair, but her knife didn't budge.

"I forget that this is your first war." Was that pity on her face? "Yes, we would have lost. The Farong would have looted the city; a few people would have been killed. The city would have been up on its feet in a couple of years. It's worse when the battle drags out for months."

I stuttered a justification.

"Poor Telora! You have been sorely used. Aghar is devious and he is well known for his schemes."

To this day I don't know if Aghar manipulated me or not. It is a possibility that haunts me. My face must have reflected my agony.

"Come, I must show you something."

She guided me towards the hill where the Gong stood. I watched it start to swing, gathering momentum. I was in awe of the instrument that had chimed the beat of our death and our life for the last sixty days. Lea led me up the hill.

"The Gong must be played one last time. The chime of peace releases the Sworn Maidens from their duty. The Sworn will leave the city tonight. Your men have not been careful with the potion and are sharing it around. In the morning there will be a hoard of men and noblings aching to test their strength."

"They would never hurt you! Not after what you've done."

She looked at me as if I were a child.

"Probably not. But the city will be sacked in the morning and the Sworn do not wish to witness. You will wish it were the Farong who were falling upon you. At least Farong have no interest in Human women."

We had arrived at the Gong. The turret was not tall, just a two story building erected on the summit of the hill that dominated the citadel. We climbed through an outer staircase, and I wondered what kind of eminent noble lived or worked under the sacred Gong. When I got up to the top, I realized the turret was hollow and that it dug deep into the mountain. There was a narrow ridge around the central pit so that someone could stand to pull the cord but that was it. That's why the Gong had such a hollow sound and made the earth rumble so: the sound resonated deep into the hill, and spread under the earth. I looked down into the depths, but I couldn't see the end.

Lea pulled me away from the pit and pointed the borders of the city-state out for me.

"Look at that," she said, pointing at the sea. "That is where the Sworn will go. Land is men's territory now." I had never seen the sea before. The expanse of water sent my mind reeling.

Lea sheathed her stiletto and I felt my gut unclench. I had not realized I was so tense.

"You are free to go, Telora," she said bitterly. "But I suggest you leave the city before nightfall. Aghar has the ear of the King and

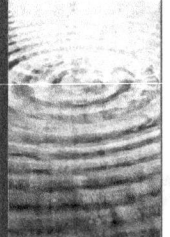

he is the hero of this war. He will not want you around to disprove his version of the story. Go anywhere you please, but not to sea. The sea belongs to the Sworn Maidens now. It is our territory, and if one of us catches you there, you will be dispatched as a traitor."

"And you? Are you a traitor?" I brushed her hand with mine. "Come with me, Lea. Let the fighting be over. I'll take care of you."

She shook her head and squinted against her tears. Her muscles trembled under her armour and I realized she must have gone without the drug for a long time. I felt for her and wondered if the pillage had left the Sworn completely defenceless. Surely, there were secret stashes they could rely on?

"Don't lie to yourself, Telora. You know why you came to me. Battle does strange things to people. I cannot live without the feel of the sword in my hand or the leather straps of armour biting into my shoulders. Does that make sense? Probably not. But I am Sworn and I can be nothing else."

I nodded. I had offered my love rashly. I don't know what I would have done if she'd expected me to stay by her side.

"Where will I go?" I pleaded.

"Anywhere," she said. "But I hear the Farong are seeking hired swords among the humans and I'm sure they'd provide the drug for you. You'd be able to take it from its source."

Lea grabbed the cord and gave it a tug. The vibration threw me to my knees. She loomed over me, smiling until the tremor passed. I realized I'd understood nothing of war. Armies were bought and sold, citadels were sacked by their own soldiers and the Farong paid their enemy to fight by their side. There was no pride in winning a battle where gold was pitted against gold. All that was left was the honour that binds fighters together, the very code I had betrayed.

"You can still choose honour," she said. She looked happy. I didn't understand.

"Join me, Telora. I'm no longer welcome in the Sworn. Maybe we can be better lovers in death than we were in life, eh?"

She jumped into the pit before I could stop her. She made no sound as she fell and I didn't hear her hit the ground. That was her due for sharing the drug with me. She was judge and witness at her own trial and she executed her own sentence.

I sat under the Gong for a while, considering her offer, but I was not a warrior at heart. Like a true traitor, I lacked the moral code to carry out my punishment.

I retraced my steps down to the city. Already I could see the signs Lea had warned me against. The men were drinking. Around me, chairs flew through windows and men guffawed, seeing how their fists broke through oak doors and crushed marble slabs to dust.

A runner came up to me and coughed a message, holding his side from lack of breath.

"Where have you been? Aghar's been looking for you. The King wants to meet you. The Sworn Maiden are leaving and Aghar wants to chase after them but the King says he can't stop the celebrations to put together a pursuit force."

I looked at the youth in front of me. He hadn't been particularly important in the battlefield, but already he was running messages for Aghar. He was beautiful, in a frail wilted way. Vaguely, I wondered if this was the man who had taken my place. I was surprised at how little I cared.

I shook my head and headed for the city gates. The Farong would be camped to the South, I knew, regrouping and making mating arrangements for the coming year. Their rut should be over by now. If I was lucky, they might not kill me on sight. ☙

Sara Genge is a doctor in Madrid, Spain. She writes speculative fiction aided and abetted by a coven of friends and female relatives. Her fiction has appeared in *Strange Horizons, Helix SF, Cosmos Magazine* and others, including translations into three languages. She has two stories forthcoming in *Asimov's* and contributes microfiction regularly to www.dailycabal.com. Her own blog is http://artemisin.blogspot.com.

don't let the revolution leave you behind . . .

Jeff VanderMeer Liz Williams Jeffrey Ford Catherynne M. Valente Alex Irvine Leslie What Robert Freeman Wexler Hal Duncan Lisa Mantchev Richard Bowes Jason Erik Lundberg Rachel Swirsky Alan DeNiro Chris Roberson Christopher Rowe Charles Coleman Finlay Marly Youmans Scott William Carter

They've already joined, what are you waiting for?

http://www.electricvelocipede.com

The Dream of the Blue Man

BY NIR YANIV

TRANSLATED FROM THE HEBREW BY LAVIE TIDHAR · ILLUSTRATION BY STEVEN ARCHER

IN WHICH BOTH A BULLDOZER & AN ELEVATOR ARE INSTRUMENTS OF AN EPIC QUEST

Those were days both terrible and awesome, days wonderful and cursed, days of creation and blossom. Those were days of great heroes and of deeds deserving of songs: those were days where right could not longer be told from wrong.

The people of previous generations, now no more than dim memories of creation, could never have imagined those days: not in dreams, not in pain, not in the wildest of ways.

If only because the people of the present generation had done so—in dreams, and in nightmares and woe.

WHEN THE BLUE man raised his gaze he saw, in the light of a sun that was yet to rise, three giant apes on top of the Empire State Building. Two of them were the hazy sons of King Kong. The third, a chimpanzee with a sailor's hat, chewed loudly on bananas and hit his two accomplices with the giant skins. The bananas passed through them without causing any harm. The building itself, gigantic and grey, was located unflatteringly on Tel Aviv's beachfront skyline. It was already leaning dangerously to one side.

That was where he had to go.

He held tightly on to the bulldozer's wheel and pressed on the gas. The engine roared and a plume of smoke rose from the chimney behind him. No one had manufactured bulldozers for more than ten years, and this one, too, was only a piece of dream-fluff one of his neighbours had agreed to dream for him in exchange for a nine-course gourmet meal. He was an expert in meal-dreaming, but there were many like him. Far too many. On the other hand, people like his neighbour, who dreamed heavy engineering equipment, hadn't interested anyone in years. There were better ways now, and dreamers with far more finesse.

And much stronger. Horrifyingly strong, sometimes, but not enough. Not for his purpose.

One of those dreamers provided the blue man with the contents of his backpack, in exchange for a special flavour, one he had searched for for years. The taste of a delicacy the dreamer's grandmother had used to prepare for him before she died, many years before the whole dreaming phenomenon had started. A year or two before, there was a fad for retro-dreaming, but it had already disappeared, and its practitioners were rare.

The bulldozer proceeded up what had once been the Yarkon Street. The surface was broken in many places—the ground's elevation had changed too often in too short a time. A light rain of frogs fell on the bulldozer's roof, stopped almost at once, then leaped back into the skies. Nameless night-crawlers thumped against the tracks and were crushed underneath, leaving no mark. From time to time the tracks passed, with a disgusting sucking sound, through pools of human sperm.

Flickering lights could be seen occasionally from buildings' windows. Once, a long time ago, this would have meant a television set, switched on. He had not watched television in . . . years. He's not even seen a set. Who needs a television when all your dreams can come true?

A naked woman stood in his way, singing horribly. He ran her over without batting an eyelid. She continued to sing for a while, but he continued on his way and the sound grew distant. The building grew ahead of him, and the concrete under the tracks became increasingly shattered. Now he could see the base of the building, erupting out of a huge mound of earth and beams, the remains of buildings that had stood there before. He pressed down on the accelerator again, and suddenly heard a hiss, a kind of sizzling sound. The bulldozer's larger arm lost its yellow colour and turned grey. He jumped from his seat, checked that the backpack's straps were tight, opened the driver's door and jumped out. The bulldozer continued going forward, melted and then disappeared.

A good sign. Another sign that whoever had dreamed the building was strong enough. Not enough to do the impossible for himself, of course, but more than enough to do it for the blue man. Very good.

He began to climb the mound of earth. Remnants of fog rose between the ruins, and from time to time a complaining sound came from the belly of the mound, and the creaking of beams, and a slight tremor. Apart from that, there was no sign of a watch, and that too was a good sign—whoever was strong enough needed no guards, no protection. His very power was protection enough.

The building had no real entrance. A transparent staircase, its edges lit by white neon, began at some point in the middle of the mound and reached up to the second floor's wall. The blue man hesitated for a moment, then got on to the

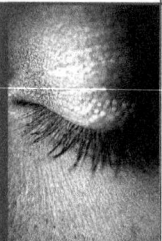

staircase and began climbing. As he did so he tried to decide if the wall was real or not. One moment it appeared solid, and in the next seemed to be made of smoke. Strange arabesques appeared on its face, eddied, grey, melted away and were replaced by others. In the background, weak and hazy, there was the sound of a distant orchestra, playing Gershwin hits. The wall came closer and closer, and with it the music, and the two coiled, and grew, and wove, and intertwined. The blue man's eyes opened wider and wider, and he felt his ears prick up, heard heartbeats, felt as though his entire body wanted to see, to hear, to contain more and more. The wall had become his whole world, and nothing but.

He suddenly coughed, and so survived.

The sharp, cutting sound had frayed the magic cords. He tottered for a moment, full of horror as the memories returned to his overwhelmed mind and then, again, his ears pricked up and his eyes opened, and he had the power, if only for one moment, to close his eyes and jump forward, straight into the wall.

No one knows when the dreams of horror began: there are those who say it is a punishment for sin, and there are those who say that humanity is always changing within. But in the heart of those terrible days there rose a man and he said—it is all because of the one, the first dreamer—he who made.

And you shall be as dreamers, so he said.

THE ONLY SOURCE of light in the grey darkness was a simple interface with two buttons: up, down. He thought about it. On the one hand, you don't dream of the Empire State Building in order to sit in the basement. On the other, it stands to reason that a dreamer, as strong as he no doubt was, would not want to risk his real body with the dissolution of the building. His counterpart in the dream can spend all the

time he wants upstairs, while the sleeping body would lie somewhere safe. Down, then.

The elevator sighed and began to move. In the almost-complete darkness it was hard for him to tell which way it was going, and suddenly he was no longer sure if he was standing or lying down. For a moment he felt a little sick, as the elevator descended into the earth. Then walls appeared and became transparent and dissipated and he could see from the building all the way out, and for one moment it seemed to him he was hanging from the ceiling, coming down from the stars to the earth, but no: he was still on his feet and around him the dreaming city's lights stood in all their awful, if not colourful, glory, and retreated from him, and the ground grew distant, and the elevator climbed and rose, climbed and groaned, towards the roof of the building and its residents, both seen and unseen.

And as it climbed so did his doubt. To achieve his goal he must confront the dreamer himself, face to face, but also reach his sleeping body. Body and mind— either one worthless without the other.

A sudden fear grasped him, and he held tightly on to the backpack's straps, to make sure it was still there. To draw courage from it. Well, he was as ready as could be, and will face whatever he met. At this point there was no choice, and no turning back.

The elevator slowed, then stopped with a groan. Doors appeared in it, their frames lit by neon, and opened. He passed through them. The lighting changed a little, and he turned and looked back. The elevator was no longer there. In its place stood a man.

"You've arrived."

An elderly man, tall, grey hair, grey suit. A hat. Above, through the transparent roof, the three apes could be seen. The dreamer smiled when he saw the blue man's gaze climb up to them, for a moment. "You wanted to meet me."

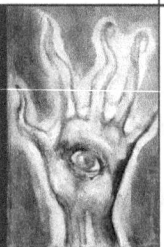

"Not only you."

"That is not possible."

The dreamer didn't ask. He looked like he received visits like this every night.

"Of course it's possible," the blue man said with a confidence he didn't feel. "In fact, you're even interested in it. You want to know why I came."

"Let me guess," the dreamer said. "You want me to dream your dead lover back for you. Or your living lover the way she was when you truly loved her."

The blue man was silent.

"Your children. You want them to be this way, that way, or maybe you don't have any and you want there to be, or you do have them and you don't want them to be . . ."

Silence.

"Money? Power? Command? You do understand I've already been asked for everything possible—and impossible."

"No."

"So perhaps . . ."

"No—you didn't understand me."

"What?"

"I mean to say—you haven't been asked every possible or impossible thing. Not yet."

"You know what," the dreamer said, "tell me. You might succeed in arousing my curiosity."

"I'm sure."

"So tell me?"

"Not before I meet your body, too."

"You do know," the dreamer said, "that I could destroy you on the spot."

"Yes."

"And you won't tell me?"

"Only in the presence of your body."

"I have an idea," the dreamer said. "Give me a clue that'd make me curious enough, then we'll see."

The blue man thought about it. "Fine," he said at last.

"And the clue?"

"I want to be God."

* * *

And the first dreamer, so it is said, had dreamed in his mind all the horror and the beauty, the fear and the dread. Seven days of creation, seven nights of invention—so some say—yet others argue that it happened in one single day, in a fit of incredible concentration. And he who dreamed had disappeared, so it seemed, from the world he esteemed, from the humans he dreamed—in his image he had made them, redeemed.

"IT'S A NICE legend," the dreamer said. "You don't really believe it, I hope." Beside him, on a white bed covered in a white sheet, lay his body, and was quite similar to him. A little greyer at the temples and maybe not as tall, though it is hard to judge the height of a man when he is lying down, and the grey murky light of pre-dawn did not help.

"It probably is a legend," the blue man said, "but that doesn't mean that it couldn't have happened."

"Really?"

"To be exact—it doesn't mean that it can't happen."

"Ah," the dreamer said. "You want dream enhancing. There are doctors, you know."

"No."

"What?"

"No, I don't want enhancing."

"So what do you want?"

"I want you to turn me into the first dreamer who could dream himself."

Silence.

"You know that's impossible. A dreamer can't change his own dreams. Even if he is as strong as I am."

"Doesn't that frustrate you?" the blue man asked. His hand reached casually for his backpack.

"I make do with what I have," the dreamer said, but the expression on his face suggested that was not the case. The light grew a little, and the shadows of the apes above became sharper, more bothersome. There was not long until sunrise.

"You can't change your own dreams, but you can certainly change mine."

"Say I'd do that—why should I?"

"Because then I'd do the same thing for you."

The dreamer thought about it.

"Why should I believe you?"

"Because," the blue man said. What else could he say? He felt a slight tremor from inside the backpack. The machine inside came alive.

"What do you have in there?" the dreamer asked.

The blue man fell silent. He didn't know what to say. The dreamer took the backpack from his unresisting hands and looked inside it.

"Interesting," he said. "Is that why you wanted my body to be present? To use a brain-scanner on it?"

"It's not a scanner," the blue man said. "It's an alpha wave generator. I hoped it would help me convince you."

"I see," the dreamer said. "It hadn't."

"My offer still makes sense," the blue man said.

"True," the dreamer said.

"What?"

"True, it makes sense. I accept."

"What?"

It didn't make sense. It really didn't. Too easy. Decisions on this scale didn't really . . .

"Stand here and don't move," the dreamer said. "There isn't much time until the night ends."

"But . . ."

"Silence. Don't delay me. Don't move! Already it took you too long to get here, and I always wake up with the sunrise."

"I know," the blue man said.

Something not right. Something didn't fit. How did he know? Where did the knowledge of the dreamer's sleep pattern come from? How did he know, with such confidence, to come here and not somewhere else? And the only decision he had

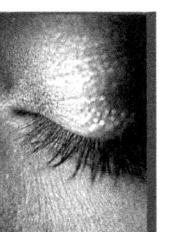

reached on his own, now he thought about it, throughout this entire journey—the decision to go down instead of up—was taken from him. Why?

"Don't bother," he said.

"Don't move," the dreamer said.

The once-blue man closed his eyes and stepped and walked and ran through the wall and beyond it and fell, down towards the lights, towards the city he had never really grown in, towards the street where he had appeared out of nothing only a short time before, he and his backpack and his bulldozer, towards the nothing from whence he came and to which, now, even before he hit the ground, he returned.

And the dreamer in his high castle upon the Tel Aviv beachfront sighed in his sleep and turned, disappointed.

AND WHEN THE sun rose over the city of nightmares and lights and fruitless escapes, there were gone from the skyline one building, and one street, and three apes. ❧

Nir Yaniv is an Israeli writer, editor, musician and computer programmer. His story collection, *One Hell of a Writer,* was published in 2006 by Odyssey Press. In the year 2000 he established Israel's first online SF&F magazine, and has been editing it until early 2007, when he became chief editor of *Dreams in Aspamia,* Israel's only pro genre magazine. He lives in Tel Aviv with his girlfriend Keren and records his music in his own studio, The Nir Space Station.

The Wordeaters

BY ROCHITA LOENEN-RUIZ

ILLUSTRATED BY ADRIAN COSTEA

IN WHICH ARIEL
IS CONCEIVED
UNDER A SET OF
MOST UNUSUAL
CIRCUMSTANCES

SHE BEGAN BY chewing on the words he left out on the sofa at night. They were little words he'd written on a napkin and they tasted of beer and peanuts and the salt of his sweat.

In the beginning, he used to write poems that made her weep. He created odd little tales filled with laughter, stories peopled with vicarious images, and pulsing with life.

Nowadays, she watched him scramble for words.

"They slip through my fingers," he said.

She watched him write short jagged sentences on bits of paper, and discarded boxes. Sometimes, he hissed through his teeth, his breath harsh and labored with effort. She listened to him groan in despair and her heart cracked under the weight of his sorrow.

WHEN THEY WALKED through the streets, she linked her fingers through his and cuddled up to him; wanting to arouse him, desiring to shake him out of the forgetfulness that made him walk like a man in a trance.

"Sorry." He said when she complained about it. He looked at her and shook his head.

"Sometimes I want to write something so bad," he said. "I can feel the words waiting to burst out, and here I am walking the boardwalk, desperate to go back home and all the while the words just keep on flowing. . ."

She knew better than to tell him what she thought about his words. She'd told him before and she didn't think she could endure another week of him languishing away beside the window, moaning about words that didn't come as they used to.

NIGHTS, HE CAME to bed late.

After the first blush of infatuation faded, she realized he was obsessed with only one thing. Still, she stayed, believing the time would come when he would wake up and recognize his need for her.

"I'll stay with him forever," she'd promised. But she was growing weary of waiting and she was filled with longing for a baby.

One night, the moon shining through her window was a bright sliver of silver fire. It fell across the covers of her bed and she saw them. They were little creatures with skin the color of nothingness; dark eyes like an iguana's and thin sticks for extremities. They crept up to her, and peered into her eyes.

Wordeaters. That was what they called themselves. They did not have teeth or claws, they did not threaten or hurt her, they simply slipped down her throat like water.

"Eat words for us," they whispered.

When he came up to bed, she lay still. She waited for the sound of his breathing, listened for his snores rising and falling in the quietness of the room.

"Eat words," they commanded.

She sat up and dragged on her house-coat. Shivering in the dark, she made her way down the crooked stairs to the living room where he'd sat all night, drinking beer and chewing peanuts, cursing as he watched the telly.

She found the words jotted down on a white napkin folded up to a fourth of its size.

IN THE MORNING, he walked through the house dressed in his bathrobe. His eyes were bleary and red, and she felt guilty thinking of the words she'd consumed the night before.

"Can't think straight," he said. He headed for the fridge and pulled out a bottle of beer.

She smelled the despair on his breath when he shuffled away from her.

"I'll be writing today." His words bounced off the walls and she caught them on the edge of her tongue. They tasted like dried up gum, but she swallowed them nevertheless.

DAYS PASSED AND she watched him sink deeper into despair. At night, she ate the words that tasted like burnt Brussels sprouts and sour milk.

"Please." She whispered to the darkness as she swallowed the words. "Please make him look beyond the words and see me."

ONE MORNING HE looked at her and she knew what he wanted even before he spoke.

He stopped writing and got a job at the local factory.

And her belly began to grow.

Inside her head, the Wordeaters grew more insistent. She developed a habit of going to the library. Wandering through the rows of books she became a connoisseur in identifying authors whose works were pleasing to the tongue.

Gabriel Garcia Marquez tasted like red wine and chocolate. Michael Moorcock was a feast of secret flavors with hints of exotic spices and expensive vodka. Virginia Woolf went down like a slice of paprika and lemon. Ernest Hemingway was tart, stinging her tongue like red chili pepper. Visions of luxurious banquets appeared before her eyes as she took in the words of ancient writers. Pliny and Plato, Aristotle and Dante. She wept as she savored their words on the back of her tongue.

She consumed a thousand literary works. Nobel Prize winners, the classics, current history, everything written with soul in it, she ate. They left behind a satisfying, nourishing taste that made the Wordeaters inside her head burp and sigh.

And her belly kept on growing.

THEY PAINTED THE baby's room blue with clouds floating on the ceiling and birds flying through the walls.

"There are words on the wall," she said.

"Where?" he asked. His eyes searched the cloud covered ceilings and the bird dotted walls.

"There," she said.

But no matter how he looked, he could not see them.

"I'm off to work," he said.

He kissed her and walked out the door.

She smiled as she danced around the bedroom. Inside her, the Wordeaters were singing.

She opened her mouth and they floated out, they populated the walls, and filled the baby bassinet with their smell of warm earth, ripening rice, wild lilies and giant tuberoses.

"Time," they said to her. "Time for the baby to be born."

She gazed into their dark eyes and felt no fear.

SHE CALLED HIM Ariel.

"Look, look how he turns to follow my voice?" her husband said. "I bet he's a genius."

He leaned in close and, cradling them both in his arms, he sang a lullaby with nonsensical words that made her laugh.

In Ariel's bedroom, the Wordeaters were waiting. She smiled when she saw their stomachs distended with all the words she had swallowed for them.

"Feed him," she whispered.

They floated around the baby, their stick limbs touching his head, caressing him.

"Pretty baby," they purred.

One by one they crooned words to her baby. They gathered him up in their arms and comforted his sobs with weird songs, and jibber-jabber words.

"Beautiful child," they sang.

The walls reflected the colors of their songs. They sang into him, blood-red sunsets, purple mountains, hazy green meadows, and the black of night.

"Ariel," they said. It was as if they tasted the sound of his name.

They looked at her and smiled.

"No need for fear," they whispered.

IN THE MORNING the Wordeaters were gone.

She did not see the Wordeaters again and she stopped consuming books.

Ariel grew fast. At three his vocabulary was extraordinary.

"Constellations," he would say. "Cosmos, curtail, constellations."

He smiled, rolling the words on his tongue as if tasting them before releasing them with a sigh.

At four he told her a story about a world where dragons and unicorns lived together in harmony. Where fairies convened with naughty imps who jumped from moonbeam to moonbeam and answered the wishes of mortals on a whim.

"Imps?" she asked. "What do you know of them?"

He looked at her with wise eyes and smiled a slow smile.

"Listen," he said. "There are stories on the wind."

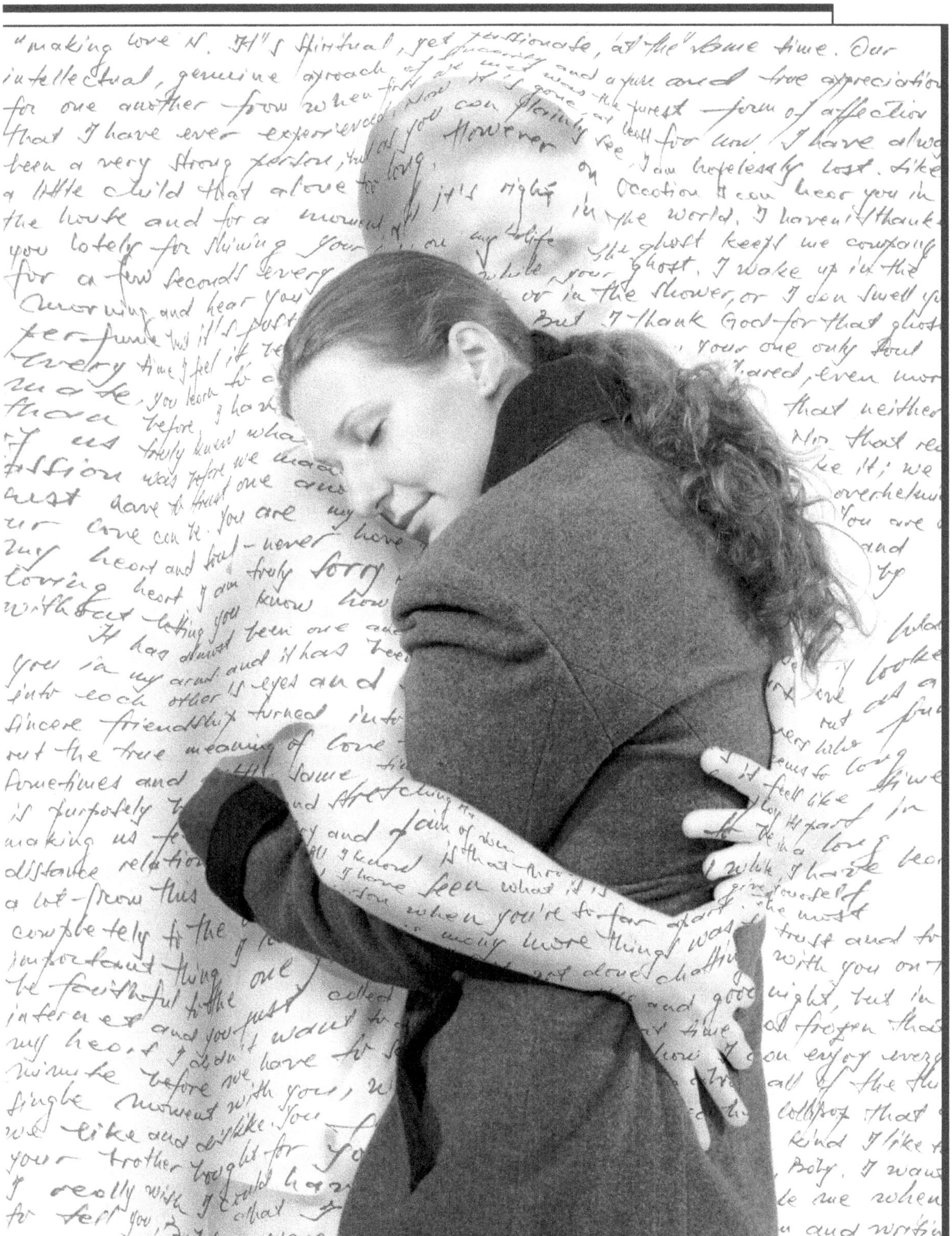

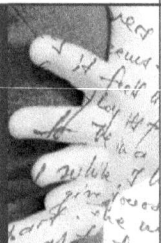

She strained her ears, but all she heard was the sound of the nightbird singing and the tall grass blowing.

"What did they do to you?" She wanted to ask him.

"Write it down," he said. "Write down my words.

And he told her a story of dragons at sunset, of winds that brought news of secret wars. His words were filled with the dreams of a thousand warriors; they were heavy with the pathos of years, and dripping with the anguish of fallen nations.

"Write faster," he said. But her fingers were too slow and she lost some of his words and his stories when she read them were only a pale shadow of what he had said.

"I'm sorry," she said, when she read them back to him.

He smiled and looked at her with his eyes that were so dark she could barely see her reflection in them.

"Tell me a story," he said.

And she told him the story of a woman who sat alone in her chair, waiting for the moon to come out. She told him of the silver sickle moon, of Wordeaters sliding down the moonbeam onto her bed, of the words she had eaten and the way they tasted.

When she was done with telling, he was fast asleep.

She held him in her arms and sang the songs that her own mother sang when she was a child, and she cried a little because she didn't know how to sooth the ache inside her heart.

"If only we could stay like this forever," she whispered. "There would be no need to say goodbye."

It was dark in the house when her husband came home. In the bedroom, the sheets of white paper were scattered around the bed like fallen leaves.

"Ariel," he whispered.

He ran his fingers over the words.

A breathe of wind fluttered the pages in his hands and from outside the window, a flame of light illuminated the dragons rising up from the page. He watched them tumble in graceful flight. Green-gold fire licked at the pages, curling the edges, turning them to ash.

He watched as miniature cities rose and crumbled; stars stumbled and collided, warriors clashed in battle, the world fell from its axis, and righted itself again, and at the end of it, Ariel was there, staring at him, his eyes piercing beyond the shell of skin to the pain beneath.

"Now, you must give birth to life," Ariel said.

Outside, the moon was a sliver of silver fire, and he saw the Wordeaters dancing on the pillows.

"No need for fear," Ariel said.

He looked up at his son.

And the Wordeaters were around him. They surrounded him with their smell of lilies and wild roses. They filled him with the scent of rich loam, the wild growing of trees and the harvesting of rice.

Images burst to life on the back of his eyelids. Warriors sprouted wings and flew away like eagles, the earth split apart into a thousand splintered reflections of itself, and the stars floated down to earth to speak with the remnants of a lost generation.

He lay there for a long time and when he opened his eyes he saw Ariel floating upward on the beams of the moon.

"No," he cried. He stood up, and tried to catch hold of his son. "Stay," he pleaded.

And he wept because his arms were not strong enough, and he felt his son slip away from his grasp until there was nothing left but a ray of moonlight across the cover of their bed.

"HE WAS NEVER ours to keep," his wife said.

In the darkness, her pale skin shone like ivory, and her body was soft and yielding under the bedcovers.

She turned her face away and he saw the glimmer of tears on her cheeks, and when he reached out his hand to touch her shoulder, he felt her shudder with grief.

"I'm sorry," he said.

And he thought of how he had shut her out, of the days turned into weeks and months of not speaking.

He looked at her and saw how sorrow had hollowed out her cheeks, and etched lines upon her face, and for the first time in a long time, he reached out his arms to her.

"WE COULD HAVE another child."

They were walking together on the beach, squinting against the glare of sun shining on white- topped waves.

"No," she whispered.

She looked out and thought of her son whom she had lost to the waves and to the moonlight, and of her husband who stood beside her.

"There are so many stories in the world," she said. "So many stories packed into books. So many words packed into libraries waiting to be tasted, and swallowed up by people like me."

"We'll make another child, if you want."

She looked at him and saw the sadness and the longing and the aching shyness that transformed him from the boy she'd fell in love with into this man with whom she had chosen to share her life.

"Tell your stories," she whispered. "Write your words and give them life. Let them be the child Ariel once was. Fill your tales with his laughter, with the color of his eyes, with the scent of his breath and the feel of his hand in my hair. Write your words. Bring him back to me."

She saw the look he gave her. Saw wonder wake up in his eyes, heard the catch of his breath, and felt the trill of his hand reaching out to touch hers.

"Let it be our memorial," she said.

A breeze blew in from the sea, wrapping them in the warmth of its caress.

"The breeze comes from far away India," he said. "Where a little boy plays on a beach of black sand and the sun is a ball of red fire."

They walked on, and his words floated away on the breeze to where a little boy with silver hair sat singing a tuneless melody under the light of the setting sun. ℮

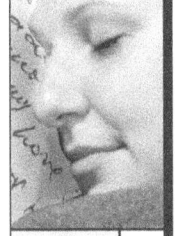

Rochita Loenen-Ruiz is a Filipina writer-mom living in The Netherlands. An incorrigible bookworm, she constantly seeks new ways to share her love for books and stories with those around her. She edits poetry for the online publication *Haruah: Breath of Heaven*, writes reviews and interviews for *Munting Nayon* (a Filipino-Dutch publication), and writes columns for Double-Edged Publishing. This story is dedicated to her eldest son who never fails to surprise her with his extensive vocabulary, his free-flying imagination, and his insatiable hunger for stories. You could say that he is responsible for the birth of "The Wordeaters." Feel free to visit Rochita at http://rcloenen-ruiz.livejournal.com.

Out of Sacred Water

BY JURAJ ČERVEŇÁK

TRANSLATED FROM THE SLOVAK BY DAREN BAKKER

IN WHICH THE
NEW EMPIRE
WILL FACE ALL
THE WRATH OF
THE OLD MAGIC

WE FOUND UROSH! We found him!"

Prokuy nearly choked. He pushed aside his bowl of mushroom soup so abruptly that half of it spilled onto the compacted dirt floor. He carelessly wiped his mouth, leaving that part of the soup that was in his beard now on his hairy forearm. He snatched up his axe and quickly climbed up the short ladder rising from the zemlyanka.

"Urosh has been found in the woods!"

The sound of axe blows, reverberating throughout the vast hilly countryside despite the falling twilight, gradually began to lose its rhythm and faded away. The men laid their saws aside, sank their axes into the fallen timbers, let loose the reins of the draught horses and scurried back to camp. Prokuy looked up. A boy barely seventeen years old was dashing madly down the slope into the clearing full of smoldering piles of branches. Prokuy knew him well. Bushek was among the few brave souls who would dare enter the woods on the other side of the mountain in search of a lost companion.

"Urosh has been found!" he bellowed from the top of his lungs.

"Stop that shouting!" Prokuy cried out to him. "They can hear you all the way to the prince's fortress! You'll wake everybody!"

Only it was already too late. Work was done for the day and the men were hurrying back to camp. Prokuy swore to himself. Another useless delay. Felling trees and floating them fifty leagues down the River Morava to the main fortress was going terribly slowly. Moymir, the newly-installed Moravian sovereign, was starting to get impatient. Immediately after ascending the throne, he decided to build a new, grand court with enlarged, stronger fortifications. He wanted it finished by winter, but here it was already autumn and the wood needed for constructing it was falling short. And Prokuy knew all too well who they were blaming for it.

Bushek came to a wobbly stop and bent forward, his hands resting on his knees. He tried to catch his breath.

"Speak," Prokuy growled at him. He wanted to get the bad news out before it reached the ears of the woodcutters on their way.

"Urosh . . ." the boy managed to get out. "In the woods . . ."

"I already heard. What about him? Is he alive?"

Bushek straightened up and looked into the foreman's eyes. He didn't have to say anything.

"Just like before?" Prokuy asked, gnashing his teeth.

The boy shook his head. "Much worse . . ."

Prokuy instantly forgot his anger and started to be frightened. Without thinking he lifted his hand to his chest and touched the talisman he wore for protection, the figure of a dog carved out of lime wood.

"Perun and Radhost, don't forsake us now . . ."

The quickly gathering crowd of woodcutters started asking, "What's happened? Where is Urosh? Is he dead?" Prokuy could actually feel the fear that was engulfing one man after the other as if one giant, dark cloud were forming.

"Calm down," he shouted over the growing uproar. "Nothing has happened! Go back to your work! I want to see another dozen logs on the bank before it's totally dark out!"

The men started muttering and calling for more details. They knew that something bad had happened. They were afraid. Prokuy shouted once more for them to go about their business and turned to Bushek. "Take me there."

But they had hardly reached a dozen paces when an unexpected cry swept throughout the camp:

"Riders!"

The woodcutters fell silent and looked off towards the valley. At least two dozen men on horseback were racing up from the River Morava along the trail that ran between the zemlyankas and the tents stitched from cow and horsehide. Prokuy froze. He instantly recognized the cast bronze helmets and plated armor of the prince's retinue. They were being led by a man of about forty, wearing a pockmarked face and armor adorned with silver. This was Vlchan, Moymir's right-hand man, the leader of his personal entourage, the most feared warrior in the Moravian basin. Next to him rode a somewhat older, bearded man wearing a simple dark frock tied with ordinary rope. A large, shiny cross dangled around his neck. Prokuy clenched his teeth. The priests of this peculiar religion, which had moved Moymir to reject the true gods not too long ago and was now forcing all other Moravians to do the same, had inspired little love among the people.

The riders rode up to the enclosure in front of Prokuy's zemlyanka. The woodcut-

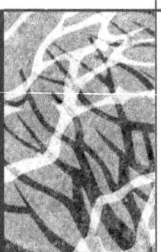

ters quickly drew back before the approach of the horses. As soon as the warriors formed ranks on both sides, Prokuy noticed another man holding back on a sturdy black stallion. He was unusually tall, bony, and dressed all in black. His raven black hair contrasted sharply with the deathly pale look of his face, which bore a hideous scar made by a deep gash. His black eyes cast an eerie look on everything around him, as if they were capable of penetrating a man's flesh and looking to the bottom of his soul. Prokuy immediately knew this was a wizard and the monstrous black wolf that obediently trotted next to the black horse easily confirmed the suspicion. Only a sorcerer could tame such a wild beast. The foreman's entire body broke out into such a case of goose pimples that he could have easily sanded a piece of oak with his skin.

"You are the foreman?"

Prokuy looked back towards the head of the party. There wasn't a trace of friendliness in Vlchan's eyes. Quite the opposite. They radiated malice and arrogance.

"Yes, sir. I am Prokuy."

Vlchan sat forward in his saddle. "Prince Moymir isn't satisfied at all with the rate of construction. And the reason for it is the raftsmen have little wood to float down the Morava."

Prokuy swallowed dryly. "It isn't our fault, sir. Evil things are happening. The men are afraid..."

"I heard. Moymir was told that one of your men was found dead in the woods, his body mutilated."

"Two men, sir," Prokuy corrected him. "Last night another one disappeared. He was found not too long ago and his body is said to be in a worse state than the first one."

"So then, there have been two heinous murders?" the man with the cross suddenly cried out and sat up in his saddle. "Surely some godless creature in the woods has done it!"

"Undoubtedly," Vlchan nodded. "And that's why we're here. Moymir has instructed us to remove whatever is holding up the swift clear cutting of trees for his fortress. It's time to put an end to these accursed witches."

"Rusalkas," a calm but bone-chilling voice corrected him. "They are water nymphs."

All heads turned towards the wizard. The tall, thin man had been following the conversation with a blank look on his face. The black wolf sat on the ground next to him and pricked up its ears as if it understood every word.

"Witches, fairies, nymphs, it doesn't matter?!" a voice called out into the subdued silence. "They're all heathens. Odious, bloodthirsty vermin that must be exterminated!"

"On that we are agreed, Bolerad," Vlchan frowned. "We shall enter their lairs and slay them once and for all. Who can lead us to the place where the last man murdered was found?"

Prokuy looked at Bushek.

"I can, sir," the boy spoke up sheepishly.

"Good. Then I want to see the body."

"The dead man is still there, sir," said Bushek almost in a whisper. "Nobody has dared touch the remains."

After everyone rushed up into the clearing, Prokuy prayed in his soul for his gods to perform some miracle and transport him to the other end of the world.

"JESUS CHRIST AND all the saints in heaven," Bolerad groaned and clenched his teeth, the veins on his ears protruding out. Even in the flickering light of the torches, everyone could see how pale he was.

Bushek had led them across the ridge and into the valley on the opposite side of the hill. At the bottom was the creek that flowed around the mountain and fed the Morava. By the time they got there, it was already dark. The moment they cleared the

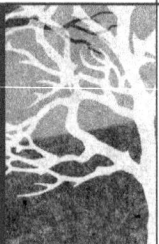

underbrush on the bank, they saw the horror on the opposite side of the stream.

Several of the warriors forgot their recent baptism in the waters of the Morava and invoked the names of the old gods in whispers. At first Bolerad resisted the temptation, but he swiftly turned away and began vomiting violently. Vlchan grimaced in disgust at the site on the opposite bank and without thinking reached for the hilt of his sword hanging at his side.

"The poor fellow must have died an unbearable agony," he let slip out.

"I don't think so," the black-haired wizard demurred. He moved to the front of the group and nimbly jumped over the creek. His cloak flapped behind him like large wings, making him look for an instance like a large, overgrown raven. The wolf followed him.

"Be careful, sir," Prokuy warned him. "This place is bewitched with nymph magic."

"Quiet, man!" Bolerad snapped at him. "Belief in pagan magic is blasphemy against God!"

"Even if some kind of magic occurred here," growled Vlchan, "it won't hurt him. He's a wizard, after all. Some people even say that the blood of the Chernobog, the god of darknees himself, flows through his veins."

Bolerad crossed himself so violently that it was nearly impossible to follow the movements of his hand. "We shouldn't have brought that heretic with us. It is desecration against God."

"He took it upon himself to join us," Vlchan said, shrugging his shoulders. "He understands witchcraft. He can be useful to us."

"Who exactly is he?" Prokuy asked in muffled tones.

"You haven't heard of Rogan, the sorcerer of the Temple of the Blood-Red Fire?" asked one of the warriors, turning to the foreman so he could undoubtedly take delight in Prokuy's expression. Of course, the name was familiar to him. Few people didn't know it. Inside, Prokuy scolded himself for being such a fool. Why didn't it occur to him earlier? The wolf, the sword forged from blackened metal jutting out from underneath a wizard's cloak...

"It's just what I thought," called out Rogan from the other side of the stream. "They were playing around with him after they killed him. He didn't suffer. They're not cruel. They only want to scare away intruders."

Urosh's head had been stuffed inside the hollow trunk of an old oak tree by the creek. Two sickening holes remained where his eyes had been gouged out, the blood around them still glimmering in the torchlight. His arms and legs were dangling from branches all about, the same as with his eyes, his ears and innards. His intestines had been bizarrely interwoven as if to create some kind of specific pattern. The empty trunk, with the ribs gleaming white from the torn flesh, lay under a tree.

"The first victim was also mutilated?" the sorcerer asked.

"No, this one is much worse," said Prokuy, approaching the stream. "It's all getting worse. First there were only amulets hanging everywhere, like bewitched knots of animal innards and the teeth and skulls of predators. There were howls in the night and flickering flashes of sorcery in the dark. But after we cut on, more frightening things started to happen. More and more of the men refused to cut down any more trees. Already a third of them have packed up and left. That is why the work has been going so slowly."

Rogan turned to look at him. Prokuy sensed that those two black eyes were sucking his brains right out of this skull. He hadn't been at all affected by the sight of the dismembered body, but now felt as if a large boulder had been placed in his gut.

"They are defending themselves," said the sorcerer. "These woods have belonged to the water nymphs since time immemorial. Their spirits are bound to the spirit of these woods. By cutting down their trees, you are robbing them of their life force."

"We realize that, Almighty One," Prokuy nodded. "We have always been respectful to them. When we got the order to cut down their forest, we tried to appease them by making sacrifices, but . . ."

"What?" Bolerad shouted. "You admit to servicing and worshiping pagan demons? You are condemning yourself to burning at the stake!"

"We shall concern ourselves with that later," said Vlchan, stemming another tide of priestly outrage. "Now is the time to deal with these creatures. I have enough men here to undertake an expedition against them. If I understand correctly, they are principally creatures of the night. They will offer less resistance during the day. We set out when it gets dark."

"Don't be rash, Vlchan," warned the wizard, fixing his piercing look on him. "Things could turn out differently from what you imagine."

Vlchan bared his teeth. "They were the first to draw blood, remember that, Sorcerer. I cannot let them kill our people and go unpunished. What you say about us doing some wrong to them has no bearing here. To me, they are only beasts that have to be hunted down."

"You can think that way if you want, but remember, this beast will defend itself."

"I hope so. They will learn that an armored warrior won't be as easy a prey as a scruffy woodcutter. Back to camp!" With these words, Vlchan sharply turned and galloped off up the hill. The men-at-arms and Bolerad followed him. Only Prokuy, Bushek and two other woodcutters remained at the creek with the wizard

"Take the remains of your friend back to camp," Rogan ordered them. "You needn't fear, there is no curse upon them. Gorya," he bent down to the wolf, "I hope you are not too tired for a little walk in the night."

As he watched the sorcerer and his silent companion disappear into the darkness of the woods, Prokuy gripped his amulet so hard that the knuckles on his fingers turned white.

THE NIGHT WAS unnaturally quiet. There was perfect calm, not a single rustling of leaves in the treetops. Two shadows moved about in the forest silently, like phantoms lost in the wilderness, unseen and unheard. These two didn't need the way to be lighted for them. The magic of Blood Fire, which transformed their eyes into demonically glowing slits in the dark, made it possible for them to see everything around them in a red-tinted light.

Suddenly both shadows stopped.

Directly in front of us, Rogan said in his thoughts.

I feel it, was the inaudible message sent by the sorcerer to the wolf's thoughts.

They proceeded more cautiously than before. They slipped through a densely packed clump of young oaks with not a swish or sound of heavy breathing and came to a stop on the edge of a large clearing. Their eyes darkened the moment they released the spell of their night vision.

The grass in the clearing had been trodden on in a very unusual way—the blades of grass were lying so as to form the shape of a circle. Hovering above them was something like a soft, blue flickering mist.

Spirits around, said Goryvlad.

Precisely the one I'm looking for. Rogan came out from behind the trees and slowly approached the circle.

They say he who enters the circle of a spirit does not survive the blows, the massive black wolf warned him. *The rusalkas will dance him to death.*

Are you sure they use a dance? Rogan stopped for a moment at the edge of the circle and looked about warily. The surrounding woods were shrouded in quiet darkness. An owl was hooting somewhere in the distance. The sorcerer walked on the

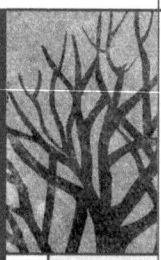

trodden grass. Goryvlad's dark silhouette crawled out from the black shadow of the trees and followed him with the poised steps of a predator.

There's a very strong magical field here, the wolf determined as it entered the circle.

Yes. And the water nymphs no doubt are maintaining their connection to it. They can immediately sense when someone enters and disturbs their protective magic.

So they will soon be coming.

Precisely. For me. Rogan stopped in the middle of the circle, tossed his cape back and drew his sword from the sheath at his side. The blade quietly whooshed and bathed in the blue light of the magic field. The sorcerer knelt on one knee, gently stuck his sword into the ground and clutched the hilt with both hands. Goryvlad sat close to him.

Rogan squinted his eyes in order to concentrate. In an instant a flare of freshly effused blood appeared and began to flow from the ruby-colored eyes of a demon whose horribly twisted face was embossed in the black metal protective shield of the sword. A blood-curdling red effulgence shrouded the blade, dripped onto the ground and quickly shrouded both man and wolf.

The sorcerer opened his eyes.

We probably won't have long to wait, the wolf heard inside its head. *We have no time to lose.*

No fear. They are already coming.

Goryvlad was not mistaken. A soft blue light gleamed somewhere deep in the woods, revealing the black silhouettes of the trees in the darkness. The light quickly grew and began to whirl wildly about in the woods.

Can you hear it? marveled Rogan.

A song could be heard throughout the woods. A peculiar song, alternating between a quivering wail of invocation and a haunting, alluring melody. Beauty and horror were wedded in it as one. Rogan felt

a slight shudder inside, something which didn't happen to him often.

Then they saw them. The lights came closer, grew bigger and shinier until suddenly they were no longer eerie phantoms, but had emerged from behind the trees in the form of naked women bathed in blue light. Half were flying about, half were dancing in the clearing—slender, fleet-footed with long hair whirling about their heads as if caught in a gust of wind. Their appearance, just like their song, combined irresistible allure with icy horror. A few of them didn't hesitate to dart towards the intruders. Rogan tightly gripped the hilt of his sword in his palms. The blood-red light began pulsating and beaming against the blue light of the water nymphs. Attacked, the nymphs cried out in pain and surprise and quickly recoiled. Their song died down and in its place the woods were filled with the sounds of malicious hissing and whistling. The rusalkas bared their fangs, heretofore concealed behind sensual lips, at Rogan. Like cornered cats in the wild, they lashed out at him with claw-like fingers tipped with long, sharp nails.

Your friendly greeting, it would seem, didn't work, quipped Goryvlad.

It isn't over until...

All the wild movement above the clearing suddenly stopped. The rusalkas grew silent, bowed their heads, and drew to the sides. Rogan and Goryvlad looked on with curiosity. Another phantom emerged from behind the trees. She also had the form of a naked woman, but she lacked the ferocity and hostility of her companions. She carried her dazzling beauty with grace and elegance and her dark eyes were full of wisdom. It wasn't, however, the kind of wisdom you see in the face of people. This one reflected the presence of things that were older than mortal memory itself. It was the spirit of these woods.

It entered the circle and stopped a few paces in front of Rogan.

"Welcome, Diva," said the sorcerer, bowing his head.

Only by careful observation was he able to discern that the eyes of the queen of the water nymphs were open wide with surprise.

"You know my name," she spoke in a voice that penetrated the body and rushed through the veins like hot mead. "And yet you are a stranger to me even though I sense some power in you that binds you to the world of gods."

"I am Rogan from the Temple of Blood-Red Fire."

Her surprise was now even more pronounced. "Ah. Yes. I have already heard about you. You are the mortal of the Blood of the Chernobog, the elected of Morena, goddess of death, bearer of the sword of Radhost. Voices borne in by the east wind have sung of your deeds. And this must be Goryvlad, head of the black pack in service of the Chernobog, who took your soul from Náv, the Kingdom of the Dead. What brings such honored guests to such a remote place?"

"I have come to ward off disaster."

Diva quietly stared at him for a long time with her dark eyes. When she finally spoke, her voice overflowed with such sadness that it made Rogan shudder. "I am afraid it is too late. Evil has been freed from its chains. They are clear-cutting our forest, burning our native land, ripping our roots out of the ground. We have been cruelly hurled about by this tempest of a new era and even though we have fought it off furiously, it will soon be strong enough to break us like a twig. What do you hope to do about it, Rogan?"

"You mustn't confront the tempest, Queen. You must withdraw before it; remove yourselves deeper into the woods. There are places there untouched by the hand of humans and will remain so for a long time. Find yourselves another home. Otherwise you are threatened with ruin."

"New home?" Diva smiled sadly. "Such a place doesn't exist for us. This is our only

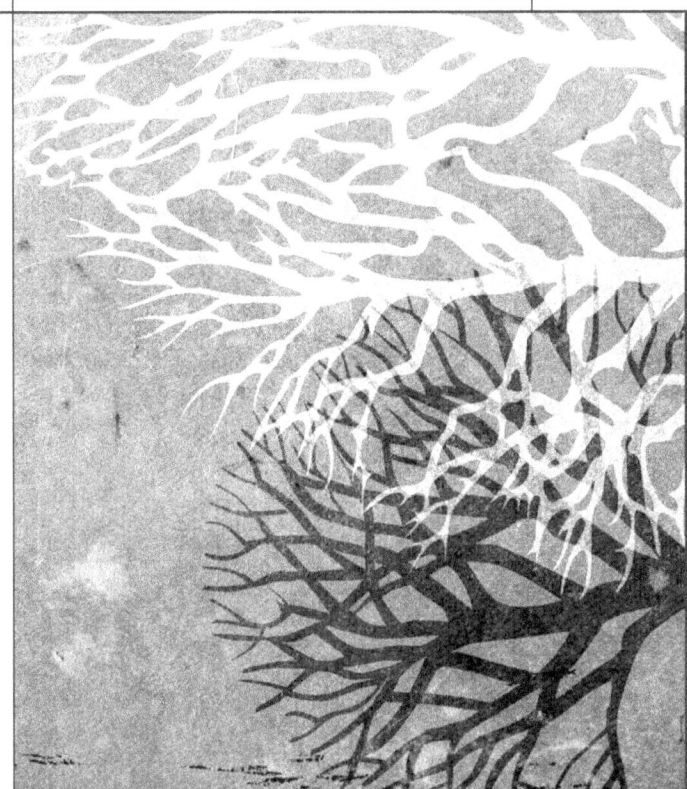

home. We are bound to these woods, since of old and forever. Come with me and you will understand. I will show you something never before seen by someone of mortal woman born."

Rogan looked around at the nearby rusalkas.

"You needn't be afraid," Diva beckoned him. "Neither I nor my sisters will attempt to do you any harm. We know how much power you have. You belong to the same bygone world as we do and in a certain sense the same blood flows through our veins."

The sorcerer rose and pulled his sword out of the ground. The red light around him and Goryvlad faded, but the blade remained covered in bloodshine. With weapon in hand, Rogan followed Diva into the woods.

"COME AND BEHOLD. This is the heart of the forest."

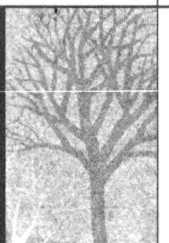

It was well after midnight when Rogan and Goryvlad accompanied the nymphs to a ground never before trodden on by the feet of man. Trees and underbrush were intertwined here to form lush vegetation, with the fallen, aromatic remains of decomposing tree trunks creating a mysterious bulwark of defenses. The ferns grew waist high and the blackberry bushes were so thick and thorny that a man could be ensnarled in them forever. Oddly enough, these remote parts, where no beaten path or animal trail had ever led, were home to the rusalkas. They were able to glide through the thickest part of the growth without touching a single leaf. The two dark pilgrims had to do everything in their power to keep up with them and not fall too far behind.

At last they reached their destination. The primeval forest opened up just enough to reveal a small lake, not too wide but very deep. It was fed by a pure water spring gushing forth from a crevice in the moss-covered rocks. The rippling water emitted a magic glow similar to that of the circle of nymphs or each of the rusalkas individually, and luminous waves of blue continuously caressed the surrounding trees and boulders. Rogan was overcome by the feeling that he was standing in the middle of a magnificent shrine. He immediately sheathed his sword.

"The heart of the forest," he repeated Diva's spellbinding words. "The sacred lake."

"The source of our life force," added the nymph queen. "The existence of the rusalkas is bound to water. We bear our children in this lake. Each of us leaves our mother's body in this water and it bestows us with magical power at the moment of birth."

The sorcerer looked at it, unable to utter a single word.

"Now do you understand why we cannot leave this place?" Diva addressed him with another one of her grief-laden smiles.

Rogan's throat began to fill with bitterness. "Prince Moymir has sent a punitive expedition against you. You have spilled the blood of innocents and the Moravians want you to pay for it."

"We killed because they gave us no choice." Diva's smile had disappeared from her face. "We have no other place to go."

"The expedition will be heading into the woods in the morning," said Rogan, lowering his voice. "Men in steel with swords and axes in hand. You cannot stop them. They will annihilate you, trample your sacred places underfoot, and after them will come dozens more who will chop down your forest without pity. Don't let this happen, O queen. I beg you. You still have a chance to save yourselves and your race."

Diva sighed and shook her head. "I know that you mean well and I feel desperation in your plea, Rogan. But our decisions are immutable. If these sacred woods are indeed condemned to destruction, we shall perish with them."

Rogan looked long at her and then looked around at the faces of the other rusalkas. He could see in them the same dreadful resolution. He glanced at a group of younger nymphs. Small girls, some of them still children, who returned his gaze with firmness and courage.

Rogan cast his eyes to the ground and shook his head. "In this case, I must return immediately to the camp. I will try to stop the expedition."

"No," said Diva, placing an arm on his shoulder. "Nothing would come of it. Even if you could hold them back, it would only be for a while. Why delay the inevitable? We are prepared. Let it come to battle today if it must. You will stay here with your companion and give us strength. Divine power flows in your blood. It will help us in battle."

Rogan knit his thick, black eyebrows. "Don't ask that of me, O queen. I cannot take part in this battle. I will not take up arms against Moymir's people."

"I don't want you to. I'm only asking for your magical power. You have enough even for us."

Diva embraced Rogan with her naked body. Even through his clothes the sorcerer could feel the heat that was literally radiating from her. The queen bared her sharp teeth. Rogan instinctively began to feel for his weapon. Diva, however, grabbed him by the forearm, removed his hand from the hilt of his sword and placed it on her breast.

"We shall do it like the rusalkas have always done it," she whispered.

The sorcerer looked at his companion out of the corner of his eye.

We're trapped, brother, Goryvlad heard his voice call out in his head. *Perhaps now is the time to summon the blood fire.*

Diva's look was a signal for her companions. Three of them dropped to their knees, then on all fours and instantly changed their shapes. Where their tiny palms had been touching the ground were now the paws of wolves. Gorya froze in his tracks and his eyes distended.

Or perhaps not...

A MAGIC BLUE light, pulsating in rhythm with a throbbing, agitated heart.

A charming, intoxicating song, the background to which at first was silence, but gradually grew louder with gasps and groans.

The touch of naked, rippling bodies, with beads of sweat and excitement.

The glowing countenance of predatory desire in eyes alternating rapidly between distended and blissfully closed.

Small teeth, sharp as needles, sunk into the forearm, thigh, chest and throat.

Heat, flowing through the arteries and veins to a thirsty mouth eager for every drop.

Movements growing faster and faster.

And pleasure, bursting forth in a loud shriek.

* * *

DARKNESS. SWEET, WEARY darkness.

ROGAN! DO YOU *hear me, brother?*

The sun. Irritating beams of light seeping through cracks between the leaves in the treetops.

By Morena's Bones! Rogan quickly sat up and threw off the black smock somebody had put on him. His naked body was covered with goose pimples. He looked around in a daze. He was lying on a bed made of moss and the silent woods hovered all about him. His clothes, shoes and sword were lying next to him.

Gorya? he inquired, testing his surroundings for a response. He hastily started getting dressed.

Finally! Goryvlad's thoughts had to cover such a distance to reach him that he could barely make out their meaning. *I woke up somewhere in the middle of the forest and no one is here.*

The same here, said Rogan, pulling his shirt over his head. He touched his neck. He could feel a tiny wound under his fingers. There was even a bit of dry blood on his wrists. He concentrated. The power of blood fire had rushed through his veins and out of the miraculously fast-healing wounds. The scabs that covered them had already withered and fallen away. *These accursed rusalkas tricked us nicely.*

Even you feel victimized? Not that it wasn't pleasant, but...

Concentrate! Svarog's disk is well high. Vlchan's party has already entered the forest by now. Can you find the way to the sacred lake?

Are you kidding? I found my way from the underworld to the mortal world.

Good. Hurry. Let's hope it's still not too late.

Suddenly the silence of the forest was interrupted by the sound of a horn blowing from afar. Rogan lifted his head and concentrated all his wizardly skills in a flash. He tried to pinpoint the exact cardinal points where the portentous sound originated.

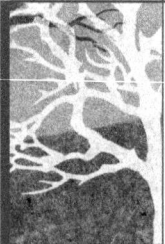

Did you hear it? Goryvlad asked excitedly.

I heard, said Rogan, flinging his sheathed sword around to his back so it wouldn't obstruct film in flight. *The signal to attack. It has already started. Quickly!*

And what shall we do when we get there?

No idea.

IT LOOKED AS if the forest itself would hinder his way, as though all the fallen trees and all the thickest shrubbery were lying in front of him as he ran along. The branches clawed at him like they were alive and ripped the fabric of his clothes and cloak and scratched his skin. Completely out of breath, Rogan stopped, reached around to his back and unsheathed his sword in one jolt.

"Chernobog!" he called out, lashing about with his sword. A swirl of rippling, glowing red energy radiated throughout the forest. The thickets began to part. The sorcerer put his sword back into its scabbard and with renewed energy pulsating throughout his veins, took off down the path that had just been shown to him.

Gorya!

I'm running like the wind!

The ground in front of Rogan sharply fell away and he was half running, half sliding down the steep slope towards a burbling creek. He stopped and bent down towards the water. He could still feel a weak magical field emanating from it. The creek no doubt flowed into the magic lake.

He then noticed a red slick in the water and pinkish foam around the stones next to the bank. He didn't need to think twice where it had come from.

He took off upstream.

THE FIRST THING he saw was a horse. A saddled horse was standing above the creek with its snout in the water. The moment Rogan appeared, the animal raised its head, jerked in fright and took a pair of steps backwards. Only then did the sorcerer notice the horse was pulling a dead man behind him whose feet were still caught in the stirrups. His throat had been ripped open with sharp teeth, his face and weapon still covered with fresh blood.

Several fathoms on Rogan found the first rusalka. Her naked body was lying face down in the creek, her insides still spilling out with the flow of the current from horrible gashes in her side. Not a trace of magical power could be felt around the corpse, the blue shine had been extinguished forever. What was lying here was just a pathetic bit of cold flesh.

He ran on. He grit his teeth so hard his jaws were hurting. Here and there he found other remains of the horrible slaughter. Moymir's warriors had slashes all about their throats, arms and thighs, all of them were bathed in blood, for the rusalkas knew very well which part of the body to strike at, which artery to sink their teeth into to make their opponent beyond all hope. Of course, there were dead rusalkas, at least five for every fallen Moravian, their bodies horribly mutilated by sharp blades, punctured by arrows and trampled beneath iron horse shoes.

Rogan's blood was boiling. When he saw a rusalka girl of about seven, her body cut in two at the waist from the blow of a sword, the ruthless part of his nature burst forward from his subconscious, filled him with bloodthirsty rage and gave his face the twisted look of a terrifying predator.

He ran into the darkest part of the forest. The treetops over the creek joined together to form an impenetrable canopy. He could hear the clangor of metal coming from the gloom in front of him. He grit his teeth, threw back his cape, and raised his sword above his shoulders.

"NO!" CRIED OUT Bolerad as he grabbed the axe in Vlchan's arm. "We need at least one alive! We'll take her to the fortress as a symbol of our triumph over the heathen devils. We'll burn her at the stake before the eyes of everyone to show the power of Jesus Christ and the determination of us, his servants, to mercilessly root out all satanic weeds from his earthly garden!"

Vlchan angrily pushed the priest away but lowered his axe. Dark droplets dripped from the bare edge on to the thigh of the last rusalka. She was propped between the roots of an old oak tree, her back supported by the corrugated trunk. Her body was smeared with blood from many wounds and gashes; her hair, caked from sweat and dirt, stuck to her shoulders and breast. She was on her last breath, but still fixed a look full of potent hatred at her enemies. Her mouth and neck were covered with the blood of at least five men whose veins she had bitten through.

"You're right," Vlchan spat out. He walked away from the rusalka and ordered four men, the last remaining survivors of the punitive expedition, "Take this bitch away."

The furious howl of a wolf suddenly descended upon the forest. The Moravians looked around startled. It came the opposite, though dangerously close side, one bloodcurdling voice answering the other.

"By Perun, what was that?" cried one of the warriors, forgetting his recent Christian vows.

Bolerad was the first to see it. A pair of red, demonic eyes glowing in the darkness between the trees.

"Our father, who art in heaven . . ." whimpered the priest and lifted his hand to his forehead to bless himself.

It happened so quickly that none of the men had time to move a finger. One of the black forest shadows leaped toward Bolerad. Sharpened steel ominously hissed through the air. The priest's head and an arm flew up through the air, splattering everything around them in their wake. Blood gushed forth from the stump left in the frock and the forearm remained stiff

for a second as if unable to comprehend what exactly had happened. The black figure then crumbled to the ground.

"Amen," snarled the man with the sword.

The warriors numbly stared at Rogan. Bolerad's blood was trickling down his narrow, pale face. His eyes shone with a demonic, supernatural glow.

Vlchan broke the silence.

"Fucking wizard. I knew we shouldn't trust you." He waved his axe in the air. "Kill the bastard."

They had at it.

The sorcerer's weapon flared blood-red and struck the first sword. The Moravian's blade shattered into hot, glowing fragments. He quickly ran his sword through the warrior's armor and deep into his gut. There was a burning stench as the shrieking man collapsed to the ground, leaving behind him a wisp of white smoke. The Moravians spread out on all sides in an attempt to surround the attacker. At that

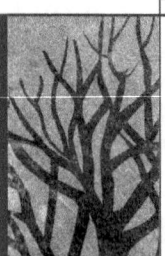

moment Rogan changed into a dark, blurry figure hemmed in by fire and blood, beyond the perception of human eyes. The second Moravian flew into the thickets, his throat sliced in two down to the spine, the third fell to the ground with one leg chopped off. The other warrior tried to escape. A second black shadow emerged from the forest and mercilessly cut him down. His horrific scream was silenced after the vertebra in his neck was crushed.

The destructive whirlwind ceased and once again it was Rogan. The blade of his sword was still clean—he had inflicted the wounds so quickly that not a single drop of blood was able to stick to it. Vlchan staggered backwards. His face was contorted with fear. If he hadn't seen it with his own eyes, he never would have believed that a man could move so fast. He knew that the wizard was no ordinary mortal, but his transformation into a murderous beast robbed him of all courage.

"What's the matter, Vlchan?" the sorcerer asked through his clenched teeth. "Lost your taste for killing?"

"Your name will be cursed forever in the Moravian basin," hissed Vlchan. "Moymir will hunt you down like a wild animal."

Deafened by fear, the warrior didn't hear a figure rise up behind him, the one he had totally forgotten about. At first he didn't understand why Rogan had straightened up and lowered his sword. When he finally realized what was happening, it was too late.

The queen of the rusalkas flew at him like an enraged fiend, grabbing him by his hair, pulling his head back in a flash and sinking her teeth into his neck. Vlchan shrieked. Diva yanked his head away and ripped out skin and flesh from his neck. Blood jetted from his ripped veins up to the top of the oak tree. He howled and pushed his attacker away, then dropped his axe and placed a hand over his wound. He tried to run away but his legs gave out after a

few steps. He rolled along the ground, making a hideous gurgling sound, his legs quivering. Rogan and Goryvlad watched him motionlessly, their eyes cold as ice. It was some time before his spasms stopped and the man became silent.

The sorcerer turned away from the dead man, put his sword back into its scabbard and walked up to Diva, who was lying on the ground. He could feel a lump in his throat when she looked up at him, her eyes full of pain and sadness. She reached out to him with her arm.

"Help me, Rogan. My strength is rapidly fading. I want the hand of Morena to carry me back to the same place where Zhiva gave me life."

Rogan bent down and took the rusalka in his arms. She feebly put her arms around him and rested her head against his chest.

"Will you take me to the lake, Gorya?" the sorcerer asked the wolf.

Follow me, brother.

They strode through a dark tunnel in the woods, as if the trees had opened up the way for them. The breeze in the treetops sounded like a distant dirge. Soon a flickering blue light appeared in the dusk before them. They stopped at the shore of lake. It still emitted the spectral glow of its magical force.

Breathing with difficulty, Diva looked into Rogan's eyes and, after some effort, smiled at him.

"We did it... We were victorious... Not one of them made it to our sacred lake, did they?"

The sorcerer shook his head and returned her smile.

"I still didn't thank you for the night before, O master of fire. We took many a lost mortal into our circle, but none of them gave us as much strength as you did. You are truly a son of the gods. And now... now give me back to the sacred water, please."

The sorcerer carefully maneuvered along the slippery stones and into the lake.

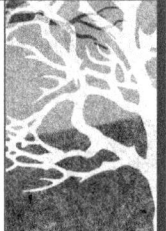

The bottom was steep and after a few steps the water already reached his chest. It seemed as if the liquid were alive and strangely washing up against his body in an inquisitive fashion. Diva stretched out her hand and let the water flow through her fingers. Contentment and composure had returned to her expression.

"I hear whispers of the goddess of the death," she said in a feeble voice and looked again at Rogan. "Kiss me before we depart."

He silently lowered his head to her bloodied lips. Her strength ebbing, Diva pressed herself against him, ran her fingers through his hair and kissed him with her last breath. Her naked, wounded body became limp in his arms. He looked up. On the shore of the lake he spotted a hazy but familiar figure. A slender, dark-haired being smiling at him with open arms. Dozens of flickering blue lights emerged from the gloomy forest and gathered around her like lost children running to their mother.

Rogan laid the queen of the rusalkas in the water and watched as it slowly sank to the bottom of the lake, the wavy locks of her hair covering her face. The sorcerer turned around and walked back to the shore. Goryvlad reared his head back and let out his grief in the form of a long howl that carried over long distances.

Suddenly, the entire lake became dark and dense and Diva disappeared from their eyes. The bluish glow instantly turned into a deep red tone. Startled, Goryvlad swallowed his breath.

Blood! The water in the lake has changed to blood!

"The heart of the forest is bleeding," said Rogan in a quiet voice.

The surrounding streams quickly became red too and blood flowed throughout the channels of all the creeks in the forest as if they were the arteries and veins of a living creature. Prokuy and his companions couldn't believe their own eyes when they saw the creek flowing around the woodcutters' camp suddenly take on the rich, red color. Even the River Morava itself turned to blood and the people living along it dropped to their knees and invoked the names of the old gods. Prince Moymir saw it from the first tower of his new regal court. He was speechless, his mouth closed so tightly that it looked like a slit had been made there from a tiny blade. He knew something bad had happened and had the feeling that it was his work. He turned away, descended the steps and ordered a servant to open up a cask of expensive Greek wine. Several hard nights, catching what sleep he could, were now in store for him.

Rogan and Goryvlad stood on the shore of the lake for a long time. After the spectacular moment had passed and the water was once again clear, Diva's body was no longer there. And with it, the magic glow of the spring became extinguished. The heart of the forest stopped beating and the magic of the rusalkas was gone forever. ℮

Juraj Červeňák is a Slovak author best known for his short stories and novels which mix elements of sword and sorcery with historical fantasy and Slavic mythology. Novels include *Warlock: The Bloody Fire, Conan And The Twelve Gates Of Hell* (as Thorleif Larssen) and most recently *Bogatyr: The White Tower*. This story is one of many short stories that feature the Slavic warlock Rogan. He also has a set of historical fantasy novels following the adventures of Rogan in the historical setting of the eighth-century Principality of Nitra and neighbouring lands.

Time and the Orpheus

BY CHILES SAMANIEGO

ILLUSTRATED BY SUTO NORBERT

IN WHICH A
STRANGE YOUNG
MUSICIAN MUST
TAKE RADICAL
MEASURES

PLAYING TRUMPET AT the Orpheus was practically the only life John Bastion ever knew. Certainly it was little different from any other life he'd ever led. The Orpheus had no band, no singer, no piano; not even a turntable or jukebox. All it had was a small dais for John Bastion to stand on when he played, a mic stand with no microphone, and, of course, John Bastion and his trumpet.

"The reason you're so essential to the Orpheus, Johnny boy, is you provide wossname, *ambience*. The Orpheus never used to have one before you came along, and these days, you've got to have it to keep what we management types call a competitive edge."

That was Barney, a one-armed, one-legged ex-pirate with at least one glass eye, who was both bartender and owner of the Orpheus.

"All a them new spots on the strip, like, say, the Blue Oyster Wagon and the Sylvian Digs, they charge an arm and a leg off their customers for the dull wall-furnishings they laughably call *their* ambience; but you Johnny boy, you give our customers something special at no extra cost. We got our arrangement, and thas definitely somethin' of itself worth a jawin' or two, an' it isn't anything these folk have seen 'afore."

Barney had first come across John playing on a sidewalk corner, all the way across the City, a battered old hat lying with the wrong side up in front of him. Barney, being congenitally tone deaf, and therefore unable to tell good music from bad, had first noticed the remarkable number and variety of people that had gathered around him; positively *magnetized* by the gawky, dark, inexplicably odd young lad with the horn, they watched and listened with slack jaws and glazed eyes. The onlookers would frequently reach into their pockets and flick their wrists with quick, sleight of hand motions, each time drawing a significant clinking sound from the depths of the battered old hat on the ground. This ritual was done, Barney assumed, each time John reached a particularly good bit in his playing.

That was the second thing Barney noticed: how John Bastion's old hat managed to draw more coinage than any other street performers' particular beat-up head gear. And that, more than the third and final thing Barney noticed watching John Bastion play for the first time in his life, was what made him decide that John Bastion was a gifted chap, and belonged inside the Orpheus.

"I haven't got nothing to pay you, other than to let you ply your trade as you know it (at just the merest percentage out of your hat, so to speak, for overhead and some such); and if you fancy a good drink, an occasional free meal, and a good solid roof over your head to keep the rain off while you play, you'll leave your spot on that corner there and come work for me at my place."

John Bastion had given him a look that told Barney nothing, and Barney thought maybe this bloke was special in *other* ways as well.

"'S called the Orpheus," he added helpfully.

John looked at him some more. Barney was starting to shift uncomfortably under his gaze, and was considering whether the addition of a bowl of nuts with each drink to his offer was worth the trouble, when John put his trumpet away, poured the change from his hat into an old brown sack, and shoved the hat onto his head, right side up this time. He sealed the sack with fray-ended drawstrings, and threw it over his shoulder, and stood there, trumpet case in one hand, sack in the other, coat on his back, hat on his head. There was something definitely odd about the lad, but when he nodded, Barney forgot all about it and led the way enthusiastically back to the Orpheus.

Barney was nothing if not true to his word, and he never paid John a single quid or tuppence, but gave him an occasional free meal, and kept a good solid roof over his head that kept the rain off while he played, although it turned out the only drink John would ever have out of the bar was chilled, undiluted tonic water (Barney insisted on this, in lieu of the rain water John initially asked for, with certain vividly portrayed admonitions concerning employee health regulations).

He even threw in a bowl of nuts.

John sat at the bar between sets and drank his tonic water, popping the occasional dry roasted peanut into his mouth. He only ate a little when he had to play. Bits would get stuck in his teeth, and, though it's never happened before, he was afraid a particularly capricious crumb would choose a good bit in his playing to dislodge and fly into his mouthpiece. Al-

though John was never someone anybody would have called temperamental, he suspected that any interruption to his playing would displease him immensely.

It was at those times, as John sat quiescent at the bar, when Barney would speak to him, giving him what Barney referred to as his 'pep talk'.

"You take 'em places they've never been, John, and could never be; you give 'em a piece o' the street they never woulda seen for themselves. The Artists' Quarter, lovely neighborhood that it is, 's no place for a Citizen Aristocrat to be seen gallivanting about.

"And your music, John, I've never had an ear for the like, you understand, but it doesn't take half a glass eye to see it *moves* them. The customers never spend a mite less time than they intend to, and, more often than not, they spend more."

He would remember the first time he saw John then, and the third and last thing he noticed about the lad and his audience, and he tried to put good words to what he thought was happening.

"Your music keeps them, toys with their imaginings of time, I reckon, and while you play, they stay and drink and flirt as though all the time in the world was theirs for the takin'."

He would ruminate over those words, pausing to chew on his lip for a moment, but, apparently satisfied with what he'd said, would say no more and walk away and return to work, or to flirting with Constance, the Orpheus' only waitress, and a pretty young thing herself.

John Bastion never thought about any of it. He just played when he was supposed to, collecting his hat and his coins at the end, usually long past time for the Orpheus to call it a night.

Then, he'd step out onto the sidewalk, standing beneath the sign of the Orpheus, put his hat in the customary position in front of him, and play some more.

One night, John ended a set the way he always did: hardly noticing the applause, the ovation, Barney called it, of the audience. He blinked the way he always does after having played an entire set, clearing his vision as though having just woken-up from a long, rather pleasant and restful sleep, then stepped-off the dais and moved to the bar.

He waited for Barney to come over with his tonic water. He didn't usually have to wait too long, but tonight, it seemed Barney was held-up for some reason or another, talking to one of the customers down the other end of the bar. John did the John Bastion equivalent of shrugging his shoulders, which involved no movement at all, and decided to look around.

He'd never actually seen the Orpheus. Night after night he would come, a quarter of an hour before opening, and a quarter of an hour after closing, and the whole time he would stand on his dais and play, eyes turned inward, lids closed, just him and his trumpet and the music, dancing a slow waltz in a wild, ancient place John could neither remember nor describe when he stopped, but which never failed to fill him with a sense of inviolable peace. He stopped between sets for his glass of tonic water and Barney's pep talk, the occasional peanut and nothing more.

Barney, as the ex-pirate himself liked to put it, could fill a hole to the center of the earth, through to the other side with talk.

At first John had trouble making out what he saw. It was like picking out stalking tigers in a dense jungle, if you've never heard of either tigers or jungles; when the tigers did jump at him he was filled not with dread, as you might expect from a surprise tiger attack, but with an inexplicable, indescribable, near-insufferable *delight*.

He saw the gentlemen in their suits and tuxedos, trench coats and jerseys and vests and leather jackets. The ladies were even more pleasing to watch, in their gowns and petticoats, their shawls and

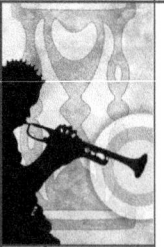

feather boas, their sweaters and cardigans. A few of them wore trench coats and leather jackets like the gentlemen (and there *were* some gentlemen in gowns and petticoats, as well), but he found it pleasing how *different* they all were, regardless of gender. He watched them gesture and gesticulate, hunching forward for a lewd whisper, or leaning back for a hearty laugh. There were little groups of silent people as well, and they sipped at their various beverages sulkily, but John found them no less pleasing to watch.

Most of all, he listened to them, all of them, their laughter, their weeping, their shouts, their whispers, their silence.

He was not playing, but somehow, he was back at that ancient place of wildness and peace.

And Constance! Watching Constance was best of all. John had always known Constance was pretty, the way a book might know a character in the story printed on its pages was pretty. But now, he actually *saw* it: she made her way through the tables like a dancer, dodging glances and lusty grabs with equal ease, never losing her poise or that joyful gleam in her eye, laughing at something unheard from a customer, returning gamely with a witty remark that could bring either laughs or blushes but never animosity or rancor (which, John realized with delight, were two very different words for the same sort of thing).

For the first time in his life, John Bastion was *aware*, and awareness, astonishingly, brought him joy and delight (two more words that were different, but were both very good at saying pretty much the same thing: which was, to be plain, what he felt at that particular moment).

There was something unusual about Barney, when he finally brought John his tonic water. Barney always hobbled over with the air of someone quite comfortable in the grotesquerie of himself, and would speak in a booming voice that belittled whatever the world could possibly think of a one-armed, one-legged ex-pirate with at least one glass eye.

It was not obvious to John, but it would have been to anyone else: Barney was shaken, and when he spoke, he spoke soberly, without the affected slur he imagined ex-pirates always spoke with, and, most of all, he spoke in a whisper.

"Drink up, John. Here, why don't you let me add a little something to your drink, give it a little kick?"

Barney gestured with the bottle of gin in his hand. John blinked back at him with that look that never told Barney anything.

"I like it fine the way it is, thank you."

John never called anyone by their name, if he spoke at all, and tonight he was surprised by his own voice, as though he'd never heard himself before, and, quite possibly, never really knew he had the knack for it. He thought about it, and decided it wasn't quite so bad, saying things, and decided to try saying some more.

"The place is jumping tonight."

He didn't know what that meant, but he'd heard it often, from customers who seemed more than passing familiar with Barney, and he thought it had a rather pleasing sound to it. *Friendly*, he thought, was just how the line sounded.

"I wouldn't doubt it. Listen, John, there's something you should know." Barney again gestured with the bottle of gin, letting the open bottle hang poised over the lip of John's glass.

"I like it fine," John said again.

Barney turned over a glass from behind the counter, and poured himself a straight. Double. Make that a triple. Hell, he filled the glass, would probably have filled two the way he held the bottle upturned like it was. This was something new as well; John had never seen Barney drink anything more than tap water when he was working.

He knocked it back, taking one large swallow to empty the glass.

"See that stiff over there? The cocky-looking one in the slick grey suit?" John looked but didn't seem to get what Barney was saying. "Talking to the giddy young blonde in the red dress."

John had to squint a bit for the tigers to come out. The blonde certainly did look "giddy." He wasn't quite sure he knew what the word meant, but he thought it was a good word for the way she looked and moved and laughed, like somehow she wasn't quite herself; "beside herself" was the phrase that followed "giddy" in John's mind.

The "stiff" was a bit harder to pick out of the jungle. Most of the gentlemen wore grey suits anyway, but it finally became clear only one of them was actually paying the blonde the kind of attention that could be called "talking to her," though a lot of the other gentlemen, and quite a few ladies, were looking as well, albeit from a distance.

When he finally did notice the gentleman, he wondered why he hadn't picked him out sooner. There was something about the fellow that certainly made him stand out quite conspicuously from the rest, even when he was just leaning over the blonde in the red dress, whispering in her ear as she giddied. Something about him made the word "confidence" pop into John's head.

He continued to be delighted at his newfound awareness, but when he looked back at Barney, he felt something else he didn't quite have the word for, though it was definitely less pleasant than anything he'd experienced before that night.

He thought about getting back to playing then, the sensation was making him so uncomfortable (he realized just then how much he didn't like that—being uncomfortable), but something inside him insisted that he stay and listen to what Barney had to say, though he could think of no reason at all why he should. Perhaps it would give Barney pleasure, he thought, and make the discomfort go away.

Barney had poured himself another glassful (John wasn't sure it was only the second since he'd looked away) and knocked it back with no less alacrity than the previous one.

"I've been 'negotiating' with that 'gentleman' for over a month now. District Attorney for the City Planning and Development Office." Visions of Unstoppable Power swam in John's head at the title, though he'd never heard it spoken before. "Seems there was a bit of an oversight when the deed to the Orpheus passed into my hands. Says it was never meant to be owned privately, that the Orpheus rightfully belongs to City Administration, and the public for which they stand."

He knocked back yet another drink, saluting his own irony.

"Apparently, it's been decided that a new public throughway is much more essential to the City than the Orpheus, and that shithead is telling us they're tearing us down, and want us out of here by tomorrow."

John recognized one of the words from Barney's pep talk, and a bright smile played on John's lips.

"Essential. That would be a good thing then." But Barney's response made him a little less certain of his statement, and he added, "To the City."

Barney kept knocking back drinks. The bottle was almost empty.

"Suppose you could say that," something in his voice sounded very much like the word "grudging" was meant for it, and John felt another twinge of delight at the realization that he was getting quite good at that, the *meaning* of things, but was brought down by Barney's next words: "And maybe you should go work for them then."

John frowned at that. He took a gander at all the astonishing things he'd become aware of that night. Looked around at the Orpheus.

"I like it fine the way it is, thank you."

Barney's look was pitying, though the effect was lost on John, to whom it was just another "look," a particular configuration of features that, while unique to other such configurations, remain the general size and shape, being inevitably made of the same composite parts, as Barney's face.

"Listen, John, I know this is difficult, but the negotiations were just fluff while the Office waited for the plans to come through the pipeline. They were never gonna give us anything. Far as they're concerned, the Orpheus is theirs, and they don't owe us anything.

"Tonight, the Orpheus closes for the last time."

John thought that over, looking around at the Orpheus one more time. The displeasure he had assumed was emanating from Barney alone had taken root somewhere inside of him, and he felt it filling him and shoving out all the delightful things he'd been feeling up to that point.

"Come back tomorrow, then."

"The City's made its decision, John, they aren't giving us an extension. I didn't tell you sooner because, well, there was never really a lot you could do about it, and I didn't want it getting in the way of your work. We only have the rest of the night."

John's face fell with all the weight and sturdiness of a porcelain jug, filled to the brim with curdled milk, and hit the floor with the exact same effect, assuming porcelain jugs could shatter without actually breaking, without, in fact, exhibiting any formal change at all.

"Well, look, John, it can't be so bad for you. I mean, you still work the street; you've practically never left it. You can always go back to your old corner, playin' the crowds the way you always have. Sure, you'd have to do without the free meals, or the roof, or the tonic water. . ."

John looked at his glass, which he hadn't yet touched, and was still full of tonic water, though slightly less chilled than it had been.

"Or me." Barney knocked back one last drink, tried to pour himself another, but found the bottle, at last, empty.

"Constance," John said, though he wasn't quite sure why.

"She'll have it worse than either of us, I expect. Me, I'm a wrinkled hand up the withered arse, if you know what I mean." (Which John didn't.) "I'll find my way, old fart that I am. But Constance? Young as she is, she's never known another life, and never wanted any other. I've always said: if there's anything stands a good chance of outliving me, it will be the Orpheus, with Constance waiting at the tables."

Barney shrugged his one remaining shoulder, shaking off the sobering effect the alcohol seemed to have on him. "But, I s'pose, 's the way of the world, and I've been wrong afore."

John didn't want it to be "worse" for Constance. And he didn't care if Barney's been wrong before; he wasn't even quite sure what Barney was wrong about then and what he could be wrong about now, but he knew he didn't want to take any chances with Constance, or with the Orpheus. In one night, he'd fallen hard, harder than any human being has ever been known to fall (and human beings, well, they can fall pretty damned hard), and he knew he had to do something, would never be able to go on if he didn't.

"John? Wake up boy, time for you to play."

Yes. That was it. It was time for him to *play*.

JOHN STOOD ON the dais like he always did, trumpet in both hands, head bowed slightly. He closed his eyes, turning them inwards, and thought of all the things he'd seen, become aware of, that night. The feel of the tonic water sliding down his throat. Barney's grotesque but endearingly familiar one-legged hobble. The gentlemen. The ladies. The giddy blonde and the District Attorney for the City Planning and Development Office. Constance waiting tables. The Orpheus and all its noise, its own sweet music; he'd never realized it before, but he knew it then; he never played alone: the Orpheus played with him.

All the delight and comfort and joy and sadness and numbness and drunkenness and sobriety: he thought them all in his head, balled them up tight and put them in the pit of his stomach.

He opened his eyes. Constance was standing at the back of the room, watching him.

When he seemed to hesitate, he saw her jaw tremble slightly, as though she'd said something. He imagined he heard her whisper one word: "Play," she might have said.

"Play."

He brought the trumpet to his lips, letting it linger there, as though savoring his first kiss; which, in the way of things that night, it may as well have been. Keeping his eyes on Constance, on all the ladies and all the gentlemen, on the giddy blonde and the District Attorney and the ex-pirate behind the bar, on everyone and everything that was the Orpheus that night, he played.

Your music keeps them, toys with their imaginings of time, I reckon, and while you play, they stay and drink and flirt as though all the time in the world was theirs for the takin'.

The first note started softly, and grew. It was long and mournful, and seemed to fill the Orpheus with its sorrow. Several hearts broke that night, but no one dared even breathe to interrupt that note.

You give our customers something special. You take 'em places they've never been, and could never be; you give 'em a piece o' the street they never woulda seen for themselves.

The bar grew quieter with each passing second, and all at once became silent. All eyes were on John as he started his last set. How many were there? Fifty? A hun-

dred? All of them were listening intently, as though incapable of anything else: jaws were slack; eyes glazed. Everyone stopped to hear the last mournful song to ever be heard from the trumpet of John Bastion.

The customers never spend a mite less time than they intend to, and, more often than not, they spend more.

John just kept right on playing, through the night, straight up through dawn; standing right there at the heart of the Orpheus, he just kept right on going like nothing in this world could ever stop him.

And everyone in the Orpheus, they just kept right on listening.

And City Administration, they went right on and built that throughway.

Now no one ever gets to go to the Orpheus; but that's OK, John Bastion thinks as he plays, because now, no one ever has to leave.

IF YOU EVER find yourself happening across that particular throughway, take a moment to listen; it's a quiet place for all the cars driving by, but if you listen, and listen hard, you just might hear John Bastion playing.

They say it's lovely stuff. Me, well . . . I've never had an ear for the like, you understand. ☙

When asked to write about himself, **chiles samaniego** enjoys using lowercase letters and the third person: "Easier to make things up that way," he says. As a writer of fictions, he wonders if everything he writes might be true, and therefore not to be trusted. He is originally from the Philippines but is currently living in Singapore.

Bleak Warrior Meets the Sons of Brawl

BY ALISTAIR RENNIE

ILLUSTRATED BY HELLSTERN

IN WHICH THE
METAWARRIORS
WREAK GREAT
HAVOC UPON
ONE ANOTHER

THE FOLLY OF BRAWL is a tower of disproportionate girth, besmirched at the base with festering lichens and nettled clumps. Venomous ivies scale its roughshod masonry. Dripping vines encircle its mildewed heights. The bloated misalignments of its elapsing stiffness represent an ominous departure from the orthodoxies of architectural form. Below its corroded lintel a single door of blanched iron offers sole access to its interior.

Lord Brawl himself can be heard proclaiming aloud from the un-turreted heights of his Folly in the arboreal wastes. The various species that flock to his abode, feeding on discarded body parts of victims, will cease their scavenging and stare up at him, blankly, as if to listen.

"My fifty Bastard Sons!" he cries, with a voice that carries through the veins of his offspring. "Bring me the living body of a chief rival. I tire of these sops of linear flesh. They are sources of amusement only: but I need the pain of one after my own kind."

It is a regular summons which the fifty Bastard Sons of Brawl will readily obey, as they travel the world on various missions, in subdivisions of two or three, hearkening to their Father's grim requests, though they are easily distracted by the allure of havoc.

"My Bastard Brood," says Lord Brawl, willing his words through the blood of his spawn. "Daily I toil in the midst of my wretchedness, but seldom am I gratified by common atrocity. I have administered every torture ever conceived, and devised many others that no ordinary cruelty could sustain. Yet I receive nothing more than the mild satisfaction of the visible terror on a maiden's face, which, at best, hardly arouses my fancy.

"Bring me, then, the living body of a rival whose capacity to endure is proof of an unbearable suffering. Do not mock me with the linear kind, but delight your Father with the most infected specimen of our stock. Head Wrecker or Mother of Peril, Hecticon or, better still, BleakWarrior will do. But bring me an idol of misery and I will show them woes that are mine and theirs in unison."

SONS 21, 24 AND 39 have proved particularly adept at adhering to their missions and, presently, have aligned themselves to a linear usurper by the name of Layman Sohk. Layman Sohk has many spies who have brought reports of a stranger taking residence in the City of Indulgences, whose demand for excessive pleasures exceeds even that of the indigenous people. The stranger shuns the attentions of Free Traders of Interest who wish to sensationalise his achievements which are, to him, the *ennui* of his removal from ordinary life. Privacy, however, often proves the mother of infamy; and soon word spreads of his exploits which, by the time they have reached the collective ear of the masses, are almost legendary.

HE HAS DEBAUCHED for several weeks and his appetite for more is like the tide that never wanes, pleasuring himself with harlots of all sexes and types; assaulting his senses with lurid concoctions; and fighting to the death with hired ruffians in the combat clubs. But he lives: and, as he pleasures himself, he feels no pleasure. These pastimes, instead, are a kind of erasure of the need to serve causes which he hates because he does not understand them.

In the private salon of a leisurely bordello, a prostitute, who does not hire her body but hires her mind, was bathing with him in the juice of stipple berries, which are full of toxins said to relax the muscles and skin. She said to him:

"Seeing as you will remain nameless—"

"I have no name worth knowing," he said.

"Why?" she asked.

"Because I might never be seen here again."

"So my memory of you will be a nameless one?"

"Do memories have names?"

"Memories have people. People have names."

"Better to forget, then."

She scooped up some stipple berry juice in cupped hands and told him to drink. "The stipple juice is full of chemicals that have the same effect on the brain as endorphins. It will make you feel better."

He drank.

"You *do* have a name, don't you?" She wouldn't let it go. It was, after all, what she was paid for.

"What use is a name," he said, now scooping up the juice and drinking for himself, "when you don't know who or what you are?"

"A name will begin to make you someone."

"But not some*thing*."

She began to massage his emaciated shoulders.

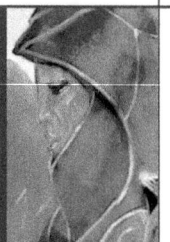

"To most people," she said, "I am some-*thing* before being some*one*. Most of them never even think of me as some*one* at all. I'd say you were lucky."

He laughed with little amusement and they were silent for a while. Then she said:

"Why do you wear those lenses?"

The Warped Lenses. She had to ask. He said nothing.

"Can I take them off?" She raised her hands.

"No." He span his head away from her. "I have a problem with my eyes."

The head-whore, who was a professional, quickly changed the subject:

"You think it's possible?"

"What?" He frowned.

"To forget."

"There are ways and means."

She sank beside him, leaning an arm on the edge of the bath. "You really have that kind of control over your own mind?"

He looked at her.

"No," he said. "Why else would I be here?"

21, 24 AND 39 WERE already intent on investigating the stranger's presence. It was, for them, a routine measure. But when they heard of the extent of the stranger's capacity for physical and mental stimulation, they began to get suspicious and, on discovering his identity, were aroused by the prospect of violent action.

It had been a while since they'd received their Father's edict and, dutifully, they had turned their attentions to the City of Indulgences, which was often a favourite hideaway for Meta-Warriors capable of controlling their random leaps. BleakWarrior had no control over his; and the Sons of Brawl had no control over theirs either. They could, however, depend on their Father's guidance, whereas Bleak-Warrior was bereft of any mastery of self-navigation and, to this extent, was likely to find himself in the wrong place at the wrong time.

Which is where he was now; and 21, 24 and 39 were about to make him pay for his shortcomings.

Outside the door of BleakWarrior's room (where he was shacked up with some psycho-slut parasite getting kicks out of some heart-to-heart colloquy), the Sons of Brawl were preparing themselves for an abduction, regrettably with some restraint. 21 was jittery with eagerness, his cleaver in his hand wavering with as much excitement as he was. 24, wielding a hatchet, was very calm, which only emphasised his talent for hate. 39 was rubbing the tip of his poniard like it was some kind of phallic totem destined to bring him additional vitality.

But when they burst into the room, they saw nothing of the woman; and Bleak-Warrior was now poised at the window, ready for a random leap. The stipple bath stood between them and steamed; and, as 21, 24 and 39 made their move (which they knew was in vain), BleakWarrior, not looking at *them*, said:

"Better to forget."

And he threw himself through the window, which exploded in a mass of splintered muntins and shivered glass, and flung himself free from the grip of his would-be captors.

21, 24 and 39 stood still and gaped, too angry even to move. Then a bubbling noise arrested their attentions and, looking down at the bath, they saw a head, gasping for air, emerge from the steaming ooze of stipple juice.

The whore who does not hire her body but hires her mind gazed up at them. The Sons of Brawl rounded on her and, with their weapons raised, vented their fury on her delicate flesh, afterwards pausing to savour the brew of stipple juice mixed with female blood, which, they agreed, was a highly satisfying remedy for failure.

* * *

*M*ETA-WARRIORS CAN *only die through acts of violence (including death by drowning, poison and fire) and are physically immune to the linear disorders of disease and starvation. They are also immune to death in cases of violent impacts sustained through random leaps, when the fall, from a linear point of view, has to be high enough to be fatal. In which case, Meta-Warriors simply fall through, rather than onto, whatever they hit, whereby the effect is like jumping into water, except that it is the body that becomes like a liquid, sifting quickly through the hard matter of the targeted surface and reforming itself as an organic whole on the other side of the transition.*

There are some who have learnt to navigate their way through what they refer to as the Intersecting Differentials of the matter through which they are capable of travelling (often called IDs, which state that the chaos contained by the material order of the universe also contains inversions of that principle). But, generally, the destination (or node) is entirely random—hence, the name: random leap.

—from *The Private Testimony of Achlana Promff, Priestess of the Church of Nechmeniah*

BLEAKWARRIOR SHOT UP through terrain that felt like a pavement. A few moments of disorientation, then . . . Nemeden, the City of Riches. He was beside the River Tho and could see the High Street squirming with dandified tourists, merchants, sooth sayers, acrobatic troupes, fortune tellers and affluent street vendors. Last time he was here, he'd stayed in a luxurious tavern that was famous for its wine selection and extravagant orgies. This time, it might be better to get out of the city al-

together and seek refuge in some anonymous ancient village in the hills.

Money, however, was a major problem; and this is where the tourists came in.

BleakWarrior slid unseen into a labyrinth of decaying streets where idling visitors wondered aimlessly—just right for being dragged into some deserted alley and beaten up for every sovereign they had in their possession.

IN A PRIVATE salon at the Palace of Layman Sohk, 21, 24 and 39 conspired.

"What shall we tell Father?" asked 21, wringing his hands like some kind of aristocratic ponce with too many gambling debts.

"The truth," said 24, ever the pragmatist.

39 agreed: "Our failure to catch the rat is only temporary. The sooner we tell Father, the more chance he'll have of tracing the location."

"Let's do it now," said 21.

"Consider it done!"

The voice came shafting through their veins like liquid ice and into their ears like a sudden hoarfrost.

"Father!" they cried, falling to their knees with fear and awe in equal measure.

"Little worthy fragments of myself, your various murdered mothers would be proud. Fear not my wrath when accomplishments are forthcoming. Though they be done by half, they are halfway to being whole; and, for this, I am pleased. Go you, then, to the highest point of your current place of habitation and cast yourself from its prodigious height. Empty your minds of all things and let a Father's guidance direct you to your goal. In the aftermath of your good work, all has been accounted for: sons 8 and 47 await your arrival with the obedience of good brothers. Go, now, and bring me the rival whose roasted bones will enthuse my grief."

They did as they were told and, within a matter of hours, had rendezvoused with

8 and 47 who, in the meantime, had been tracking BleakWarrior who, in the meantime, too, had been well aware that he was being tracked.

NAILER OF SOULS was face to face with a Meta-Warrior of growing renown called Be My Enemy. She was taunting him with verbal abuse that had about as much effect on him as flecks of dust against the void.

"Your ugliness resembles the facial contortions of a hog at the slaughterhouse," she spat. "You have the elegance of a bat with its ears removed. If I were forced to love you I would cut out my heart and feed it to the dogs to please me better. Tell me, Nailer, do you sleep in the sewers of the linear folk? Why else would your robes stink so forcibly? I would likely vomit if it weren't for the fact that you disgust me so much."

Finally, she leapt, spider-like, towards him, her flails raised, one in each hand, ready to slam with precision into his temples. It was her favourite move against Meta-Warriors with big reputations. She liked symbolism, which was the basis of the reputation she was trying to build now.

But Nailer of Souls responded as if he was made of air rather than flesh. His club, spiked with a single nail, swung up in an arc and impaled itself in the underside of her chin.

It was the best piece of symbolism Be My Enemy had ever seen.

She had failed, having counted on speed. Nailer of Souls had counted on the will to be faster. Her tongue had been pinned to the roof of her mouth; her teeth had been shattered; and, more to the point, her mouth had been shut. When the Nailer removed his weapon, she fell limply to the ground, too stunned even to whimper.

Nailer of Souls bent over her and, reaching into her body, dragged her soul from its containment of flesh, proceeding to devour it in a series of gulps that resembled a gannet scoffing a speared fish. Be My Enemy's belated scream was of untold

desperation compared to the physical pain she'd received from the force of the blow.

As Nailer of Souls stood enjoying the moment of resuscitation, he suddenly caught a whiff of some ghastly concentration of bitter and twisted life essences, against which the soul of Be My Enemy had smelt positively sweet. He raised his head at an angle and sniffed, filling his lungs with definite traces of putrescent anima. And there was one among them, too, full of agonies too deep to conceive, even more infested with rot than the others.

Drooling at the mouth, Nailer of Souls walked to the cliff edge of the hill upon which he had slain Be My Enemy, and leapt. He followed the stench through a maze of IDs, which led him, in the end, to a place he disliked more than most.

Nemeden.

He had emerged on the outskirts of the city, and the smell was coming from well within its intricate clusters of marble domes and minarets.

But it wouldn't take him long to get there, not even by linear means.

THE FREE TRADERS of Interest spoke of a highly unusual spree of violence which had resulted in the deaths of two visitors to the city and the serious injury of six others. Nemeden had never known anything like it. Among the victims were men and women of all ages, beaten and robbed within a space of four hours during an average market-day afternoon.

The killings were to some extent regrettable because they tended to attract attention in linear societies where law enforcement was more advanced, but they were necessary due to the dangers of being recognised (two of his targets had caught a glimpse of the Lenses, while the others had been more efficiently dealt with). They had served their purpose, however; and Bleak-Warrior now had the means for financing his stay in a private residence of considerable luxury.

One useful effect of the killings was—precisely—to ensure that the City Arbiters were especially vigilant, which meant that the Sons of Brawl, much against their habitual tendency, would be forced to tread carefully in mounting their attack. It was in the interests of Meta-Warriors to keep a low profile in places like this—places where they'd be regarded and pursued as freaks rather than embodiments of Nature. There were already one or two linear humans or groups who'd made certain discoveries about the presence of "unusual visitants", but who were luckily too wary of the repercussions (the accusations of craziness or eccentricity) to be profligate about voicing opinions of the facts. Because of that, they (some of them known personally to Meta-Warriors) had determined to take a more secretive course in widening their investigations, tending to form clandestine academic factions or mysterious sects reported to be engaged in queer religious practices.

BleakWarrior knew one of them himself—a priestess from the Church of Nechmeniah—who had gained his confidence and, on one occasion, had even helped him. But Achlana Promff couldn't help him now; not now that there were five of the Bastard Brood on his tail. There was nothing for him but to knuckle down and face up to the fight. The Sons of Brawl were hardly versed in the arts of diplomacy: but, then again, neither was he.

IN THE PRELIMINARY stage of his existence, BleakWarrior wanders over a vast and vacant territory of desolate hills and staggered peaks, where granite cresses overhang the marshy fens and discoloured summits elapse into long ridges of twisted rock. Storms rage and abate over a dreary terrain where rain ravages the foremost heights and sinks to a heavy pelt in the lower braes. No living creature, warm- or cold-blooded, could withstand the conflagration of raw conditions, that to the mind and body bring dreadful hardships, with-out resorting to a savagery that rivals the hostilities born against it. And, for this reason, BleakWarrior is wild; and wilder still because of the all-too-seeing sight—the penetrating gaze of the Lightning Vision—that enables him to see the supernatural aspect of the natural world, where the metaphysical hues of physical reality are as clear to him as corporeal objects.

It is the world outside of linear time, where an eternal stupor of elemental forces manifest themselves as distorted beasts that war without pause or as feasting deities too beautiful or strange to gaze upon. Ghosts and denizens populate his vision with terrors and splendours; celestial figures dance naked over the glowing heaths: and, for all his sense of fear and wonder, BleakWarrior cannot conceive of them without going mad.

EONS HAVE PASSED, and BleakWarrior is drawn from the world of excessive marvels by the ululations of a harp that trails on the wind like the residue of sorrow. It is the music of the Bard who, when approached, does not open his lips to speak, but on his harp invokes the utterance of words:

"One who wanders, from your madness now afforded some relief, the timbre of my strings has reduced your visionary convulsions to a material calm. My bardic offerings have delivered you from your impressions of lunacy. Come sit by the blaze of my hearth and slake your thirst on the draughts my naiads bring."

BleakWarrior sits and drinks. The Bard affixes the Warped Lenses.

"Your restricted madness compels you to a mastery of your senses, which is all the more ferocious for its underlying dereliction. This, your weakness, now your strength, to enemies will convey their bodily ruin; and to you will bring your dedication to their doom."

IT WAS TIME. The freshness of the morning before sunrise would keep his instincts

keen. The streets, by and large, were deserted. East of the market square lay a clutter of alleys and arcades that would provide a sufficient territory for secluded combat.

He didn't have to search the shadowed nooks to know that the Sons of Brawl were following his progress through the maze of ancient conurbation. And as he rounded the bend of a long and empty street, crammed to the heights with intersecting layers of Fiddithian and Mharothic architecture, they were there, five of them, waiting for him with weapons poised.

BleakWarrior approached and made a ritualistic motion that was his personal prelude to battle. Finally, he drew his Weapon of Choice, which flew from its sheath with an ominous ring of honed steel.

The Dirk.

And holding it clasped in both hands, with his legs apart and arms outstretched before him, BleakWarrior bade the Bastard offspring do their worst.

"Nay, BleakWarrior," declared 24. "You will receive a good beating at our hands, but you will live to suffer much greater torments at the hands of our illustrious patron."

"Best lay down the Dirk," added 39, "which will soon be ours by virtue of our victory. Lord Brawl awaits your company with anguishes contrived at your expense."

BleakWarrior's frown only deepened and the ripple of his brow increased.

"Waste not your words on speculative discourses," he said, "which have no root in the decisive consequences of action. The Dirk and I have other plans concerning the distribution of pain between us."

But as BleakWarrior prepared himself for an onslaught, he saw behind the Sons of Brawl a figure glide with ethereal swiftness out of the gloom. Sensing an untoward presence, the Sons of Brawl turned to look; and their faces, suddenly, bore the expression of their shattered bravado.

"Nailer of Souls!" gasped 21.

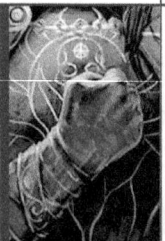

And a long silence passed between them; and Nailer of Souls was almost within striking distance when 24 took courage and said:

"There stands a confluence of miseries no duty to our Father can allow us to deny. Good brothers, take heart. We have pursued a rat and discovered a Mastodon. Think of our Father's joy when such a prize falls wrapped in blood into his lap. Cripple him but do not kill!"

The instruction given, the Sons of Brawl pounced on their prey, but the match was one of saplings to a hurricane. Nailer of Souls went about his business with chilling elegance, stealing among them with ease and with an exactness in every parry and stroke that struck asunder the Bastard host.

Yet the Bastards were no novices. Their adroit ferocity allowed them to avoid the more precipitous blows of their adversary. Desperation, too, played its part. Empowered to bravery through the reflexive impetus of sheer panic, 21 embarked on a rolling manoeuvre that enabled him to clip the calf of Nailer of Souls with his jagged-edged cleaver. The Nailer lost his balance by an inch or two—not much. But it was enough to rouse the Bastards to a less evasive approach in coping with the Nailer's deftness.

BleakWarrior, meanwhile, saw that the time was ripe for his discreet withdrawal from the melee. There were no obediences to codes of honour in the world of universal strife. Far better to let Nailer of Souls indulge his hunger for souls composed of cosmic filth, for he was not to be challenged when newly revived by their nutritious boons.

But a rational acceptance of the risks involved was not a thing to motivate Bleak-Warrior; nor was it courage that determined his actions: it was madness that defined him, and it ran in his veins with unstoppable motion like a river in spate.

21 was the first to fall. BleakWarrior

slit open the back of his neck and felled him like a sacrificial ox. 39 came next. BleakWarrior planted the Dirk in the small of his back, causing him to crumple like a burning leaf.

The confusion caused by his appearance played into the hands of Nailer of Souls, who promptly smacked the jaw of 47 with the butt of his club and sent him spinning. Number 8 made the mistake of seeing this as an opportunity to make a move. He swung his studded cosh towards the Nailer's upper body with all the force he could muster. But the Nailer dropped himself to his knees and lowered his head—the cosh passed over him—then sprang to his feet and delivered an almighty thwack into number 8's groin.

8 went up, then down and didn't rise. The Bastard's candle had been snuffed.

BleakWarrior, meanwhile, was busying himself with 47, whose jawbone had been unhinged like a piece of machinery. It seemed appropriate to BleakWarrior that he should tear it off completely from the Bastard's face. So he took a grip of 47's chin and wrenched it sideways with all his strength. A few vicious twists accomplished the deed, and it was good to hear the Bastard squeal like a puppy roasting on a spit.

And now the Nailer was closing in on 24, and there was nothing 24 could do about it except die.

Accordingly, the Nailer leapt into the air and turned like a bird on a swirling eddy. The club, spiked with a single nail, impacted almost with delicacy into 24's forehead. 24's body wilted with an instantaneous limpness like a piece of string.

BleakWarrior wasted no time as the Nailer endeavoured to prise his weapon from the perforated skull of 24. He charged full on, ready to slam the Dirk into whatever part of the Nailer's body presented itself first. But Nailer of Souls turned to meet him with an unpredictable rippling of his form. He caught BleakWarrior's arm and stayed the Dirk, then span low and buried his head in BleakWarrior's abdomen. BleakWarrior felt himself being hoisted and twirled; and the Nailer dumped him onto the ground like a man offloading a heavy sack.

BleakWarrior wanted to struggle to his knees, but a foot on his back pinned him to the cobblestones.

He knew it, then, that he was going to die.

Badly.

I*T IS WRITTEN* in *The First Book of Absolutes that the soul is a derivation of the Fundamental Awe of Nechmeniah when first she developed an awareness of herself as the Over-Notion of Existence and Time.*

As practitioners of the Church of Nechmeniah, it is our belief that we are able to receive the same extreme of realisation whenever we encounter new things or experiences that appeal to the Fundamental Awe in all of us. Crucially, however, the arousing freshness of these encounters is brief because of their obfuscation by the degrading animal distractions that characterise our physical condition. Needless to say, a sustainable Awe is recoverable through death, whereupon our souls are re-absorbed by the primacy of the Life Before the Body.

But my visitor tells me that this is wrong.

Instead, he says, we are strictly bound to a material existence that has no root outside of itself. Anything that exists beyond the reach of our senses is but a part of the expansive interaction of all things operating as a contingent body of differential states. What cannot be seen can be felt, he says, which makes all things, mental or physical, equally real. Some substances

are less palpable than others—that is all. And, to this extent, the body and soul are a single unit consisting of extremes of materiality which cannot exist in dualistic separation.

The soul, he says, is a metaphysical extension of the physical order of the body which, in turn, is a physical extension of the metaphysical chaos of the soul: to segregate one from the other is to obliterate both, and to extinguish the flame of Life.

Forever.
—from The Private Testimony of Achlana Promff, Priestess of the Church of Nechmeniah

THE HAND OF the Nailer slipped into BleakWarrior's flesh as if through liquid. BleakWarrior's sense of selfhood seemed to fold in upon itself, to implode upon an internal core of gravity so strong that it must shrink to a material density.

It did.

And the Nailer wrapped his fingers around it and began to manipulate it from its home of flesh; and the feeling—not of pain—was akin to having the viscera removed through some powerful means of vacuum suction.

BleakWarrior squirmed like a maggot on the end of a stick. He tried to scream, but his power of utterance was utterly lost. His eyes, too, were beginning to fail. The last thing he saw was the Nailer leaning over him with his mouth ajar and slavers dangling from his lips.

BleakWarrior was being drawn out of himself, and the sensations were awful, like being sucked through a miniscule abyss, but in reverse, as if the abyss were being sucked through him.

With an unusual lack of suddenness, however, the Nailer began to recoil from BleakWarrior's degenerated physique, as if someone or something were pulling him away. All at once, he released his supernal

grip on the soul of BleakWarrior and, more suddenly now, keeled over as if struck on the face by a blunt object.

BleakWarrior felt his inner vitality return to the entire compass of his being with renewed vigour. He had sampled aphrodisiacs that had given him a similar injection of desperate urgency.

But not like this.

The smoothness and speed of his movements were such that he didn't fumble for the Dirk where it had spilled from his hand during the course of his fall. He whipped it up nimbly and rolled to his feet. Nailer of Souls was sprawling before him, coughing and spewing and gasping like a man brought back from the brink of drowning. BleakWarrior grabbed the Nailer by the hair and drew his head back so that his throat was exposed to the ruminations of the Dirk.

"Nailer of Souls," he said, "how came you to abandon your efforts to devour me? It makes no sense in the eyes of the Dirk and me."

The Nailer's eyes rolled as he unloosed his tongue to speak:

"Your soul to me is poison, BleakWarrior. It has reduced my thirst to a sickening repulsion. I am desolate, yes, and I feed on the desolation of others. But your madness is a toxin in the blood of my being I cannot endure.

"You have me within range of the Dirk, BleakWarrior. I have a mind that the Dirk and you will satisfy my drooth, forever."

"Then since you are about to die," said BleakWarrior, "tell me what you know of our uncommon purpose. What are we, Nailer? And *why*?"

"We are what we are, BleakWarrior— no more, no less. I am the manifestation of the desolate mood that underpins me. You are the embodiment of the madness that empowers you to your probable doom. We are the physical expression of natural states that serve no purpose beyond their immediate function."

"But surely a strain of consequence must bind our absent purpose to some singular aim."

"Must the wind blow for a specific reason?"

"I am stirred too much by wafts of madness to swallow this."

"The wind is free to swallow anything."

"None of this conveys an answer," said BleakWarrior. He pressed the Dirk against the Nailer's throat.

"It is all the answer I can give."

"Then the Dirk compels me to erase your life in bitter haste."

BleakWarrior drew the Dirk across the Nailer's throat with a swift incision that splashed blood across the cobbles freely as wine. He let go of the head and watched it fall to the stones with a delicate smack. He gazed upon the face of the Nailer. The expression he saw was more of relief than pain.

Tears were seeping under the Warped Lenses of BleakWarrior when he sheathed the Dirk and stepped from the bloody pool that welled around his feet. The trail of gore he left behind him subsided by degrees as he departed from the scene of the melee. A sudden urge to rip the Lenses from his eyes—to immerse himself in the thralls of madness—rose up in his gorge like a volcanic spume. But it was quickly dispersed by the exultant thought that, by not knowing who he was, not knowing what he was, he would kill to find out.

Or die trying. ☙

Alistair Rennie was born in the North of Scotland and now lives in Italy. He has published short fiction in *The New Weird* (Tachyon), *Fabulous Whitby* (Fabulous Albion), *Electric Velocipede* and *Shadowed Realms*.

The WEIRD FILMS of BILL PLYMPTON, OPTIMIST

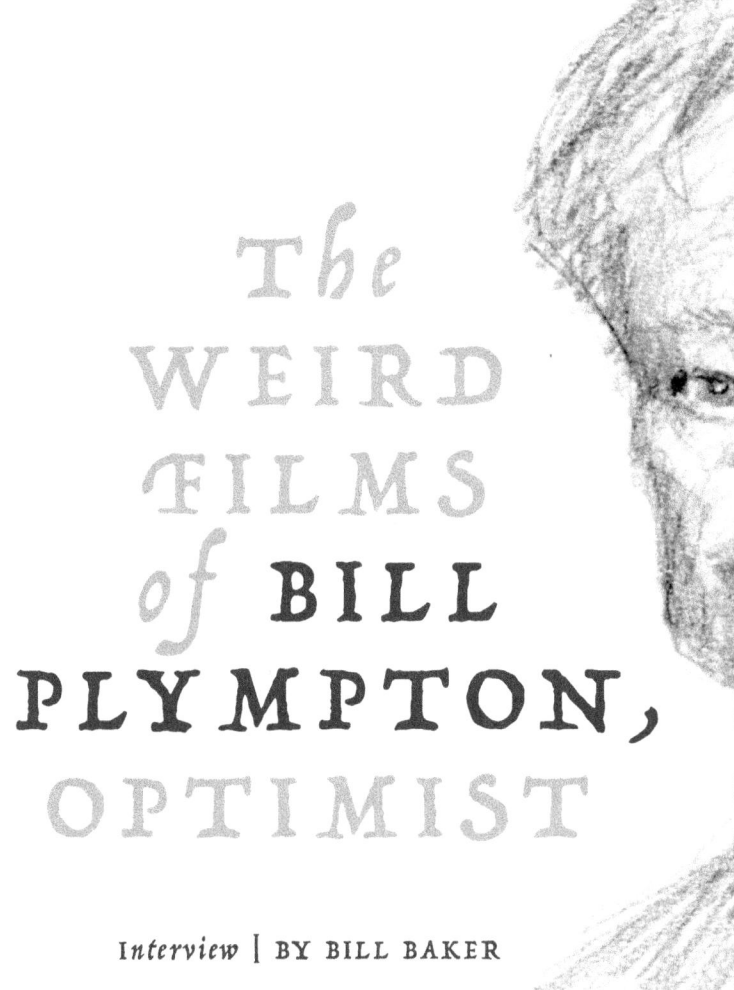

Interview | BY BILL BAKER

B ILL PLYMPTON HAS *been making strange animated films for the better part of a generation now. His short-form stories, like the Oscar-nominated musical metamorphosis "The Face," ranked among the highlights of MTV's 1990s anthology shows* Cartoon Sushi *and* Liquid Television; *his full-length 1997 feature* I Married a Strange Person, *about a man whose every daydream becomes reality, has become a bona fide cult classic. Quirky, otherworldly and idiosyncratic, yet always entertaining and accessible, his work has garnered both critical praise and a devoted fanbase—not to mention a place* on Weird Tales's *own list of "The 85 Weirdest Storytellers of the Past 85 Years" [March/April 2008].*

November will see the release of a new book, Through the Wire, *in which Plympton illustrates twelve songs by the hip-hop musician Kanye West.* Weird Tales *correspondent Bill Baker caught up with Plympton this summer during the release of his latest animated feature,* Idiots and Angels, *to quiz him about his creative process, why he still draws every frame of his cartoons himself, and how a simple stroll around his neighborhood in the Big Apple often turns into a walk on the weird side.*

Your new animated film, *Idiots and Angels*, is out now. Where'd that come from? Well, I don't know where the original idea came from, and usually I do. But the first reference I can remember was three years ago at a [film] festival in France, in Lille. I was walking with this guy to my hotel, and he asked me what my next film project would be and, off the top of my head—I don't know where it came from, it just seemed appropriate—I said, "An asshole wakes up one morning with wings on his back."

And he said, "Yeah. Hey, that's a good idea." So that night, as I laid in my hotel room, I actually started doing preliminary sketches, story ideas, character designs, possible plot devices, and it just felt like it was really something that would be fun to make, and could be popular with the audience.

You said you normally do know where your ideas come from. Do they arise from striking images, or perhaps concepts, you've encountered? Usually, it's something that I observe. I live in New York City, and it's kind of a cartoon city, so I see a lot of bizarre events and people, and hear a lot of bizarre stories. For example, the *Guard Dog* series was inspired by an event I saw in the park right by where I live. It's called Madison Square Park, and I saw this dog barking at a little bird. And I wondered, why is a dog threatened by this tiny, little birdie? So I went inside the dog's brain and realized . . . well, I didn't *realize*, but made up this fantasy that the dog was afraid the bird would attack his master, and he would lose his meal ticket. So, that was the inspiration for *Guard Dog*, and that whole series has become very successful—and all simply because I looked at something that's an everyday occurrence, and I needed an explanation [for it]. There're so many things in life that are just mysteries. And oftentimes, by exploring these mysteries, I get a lot of good ideas.

Also, a lot of my ideas come from seeing something that's confusing. You overhear a conversation, and you don't hear the whole conversation, you hear a clip of it. And so you sort of add words of your own to it, or misinterpret what they're saying, and it's so surreal, so absurd, and so bizarre that it works. It becomes a plot for your next short film. So it comes in many different ways.

Also, sometimes I'll just lie in bed in the morning for an hour and just let my mind wander. I think daydreaming is very important part of my creative process, and often my mind will sort of take flight and touch on these bizarre ideas, and I write them down as I think of them. And, before you know it, I have a plot for a new film.

So rather than being purposefully weird or quirky to be funny, these are expressions of your take on the world, and represent your own particular world view. Yeah, real life. These are the kinky side of life, the bizarre side of real life.

When it comes to your animation work, you've always insisted on drawing every single frame yourself. Yeah, I do. There're three reasons for that. One is that it's quicker. If I had to hire somebody to do it, I would have to keep correcting them, and so I find it faster to do it myself. Number two, it's cheaper. Rather than hiring other animators . . . The good ones are very expensive. You know, like a thousand dollars a day, or whatever. I just don't have that kind of money. And number three, it's more fun. For me, the pleasure of making these films is to do the drawings myself. That's what I want to do. I don't want to be a big boss, or a bureaucrat, or a producer. That's boring. I want to be the guy doing the drawings, and making up these characters, and having them move around.

Plus, you're investing a big part of yourself directly into the film. Yeah . . . You know, my films aren't hugely successful, I'm not like Pixar or anything like that, but they're fun for me to do, and they're quirky, like you say. They have their own sort of "Plympton look." It's sort of a brand now. I have a kind of a cottage industry, making these animations, and I like it like that. For me, that's comfortable. I have no pressure. I have no deadlines. I have no marketing people, or toy companies pressuring me to finish it at a certain time. So, it's a very easy lifestyle for me, and I'm just blessed that I can make money on these films, and I just turn them out whenever I want.

At any given time, while you might be working on something longer like *Idiots and Angels*, typically you're simultaneously working on one or two shorter films, as well. How do you manage to juggle all that—and why do it that

way? Does it help keep you and the work fresh? Yeah, that's part of it. Although when I was making *Idiots and Angels*, I pretty much concentrated on the feature, unless I had a deal [come up]. For example, I was working on a music video for Kanye West, and that was a real rush job, so I had to sideline the feature for that. But the shorts that I do ... *Shuteye Hotel* was done before production of *Idiots and Angels*, and then *Hot Dog* was done after production. So, when I'm drawing, that's pretty intense. That's ten, twelve hours a day, seven days a week. And I get in this real zone. It's almost like a high, and I'm so single-minded about finishing this film, about the characters in the film, and the storytelling in the film, that's it hard for me to get distracted by other projects. In fact, I refuse to be distracted, unless it's a big commercial or something.

You know, I just remembered another little story. *Shuteye Hotel* ... that was a real Edgar Allen Poe-ish kind of story, and it was interesting because that idea came from a visit to another hotel while I was at another foreign film festival. And I remember waking up in the morning, and this pillow, this very plush pillow that I'd been sleeping in was so deep and so plush that it had encompassed my head. And I thought, "Oh my god, this pillow is trying to eat my head!" And right there, I just knew that was a good idea for a film.

So *Shuteye Hotel* is basically a murder mystery where this pillow is eating everybody's head that lays on it. And I thought that was such a fun idea. It's very Hitchcockian, you know? It's like there's this mysterious murderer, you don't know who it is, and then you realize that it's a very soft, comfortable pillow who's taking revenge on people for drooling on them, and fluffing them up and having pillow fights. I'd like to extend that idea, because I think pillows can be very scary creatures.

How would you describe your general creative process? Well, for example, with *Shuteye Hotel*, I will do a lot of sketches of what the hotel looks like, what the pillow looks like. I will try and find a resolution, like the discovery that the killer is actually a pillow, and I save that for the last because that is the gag, that's the punch line. And I wanted this killer to be, in the imagination of the audience, some vicious strangler or rapist or psychopath or something like that. I build on that plot device of unmasking the killer. So, I'll write down possible story ideas, or gag ideas, or possible killers that could be false trails, that sort of thing. I just play with it, and think about it. I close my eyes and just imagine: what would be fun to put in there? What would really be cool? What would the audience really like to see in the film?

Once I have a basic concept for the plot, I start storyboarding. The storyboarding process is a very important process for me, because that really defines so much of the film in terms of what the characters look like, the atmosphere, the pacing, the storytelling, the cutting, the camera work, the camera angles, the lighting, the shading. And once I have a good storyboard, then I start doing layouts—taking every shot and defining what action takes place in that shot. For example, if it's the woman fighting with the pillow, the cop fighting with the pillow, then I show the first sequence and the last sequence, so I know what takes place in that shot.

Then I go ahead and start making the animation. And the animation is, obviously, the longest part, because each drawing has to be drawn by me. For a short film, that will take two or three weeks, something like that, to do all the animation. I'll do the backgrounds while I'm doing that. And then, I hand it over to my staff, and they will scan it, and clean the drawings, and composite the drawings, and sequence the drawings, and color the drawings. That's a very important part; that's basically putting it all together. And then, once we have all the shots assembled, and colored, and completed, we edit the film together. Generally, I don't use dialogue for my films ... so we just put in sound effects and music, and that's it.

You said the storyboards are very important to your overall process. How detailed are those? Because when one sees most film storyboards, you clearly can tell what's going on, but it isn't necessarily that detailed an image. For *Idiots and Angels* it was very detailed, simply because it's a big film. I did, I think, 220 pages of storyboards—six storyboards per page. So it's almost a drawing

for every frame of the film. And [in the end] it will be published as a graphic novel.

You really can't get a truer print vision of the film than that. Right. And it's good for young animators to see how the process works, how my storytelling works, the difference between storyboards and the finished film. It's very instructive. A lot of schools buy my books, my graphic novels, for that reason alone.

Who's influenced you? Well, there are a lot of people. Of course, Disney was the first huge influence, as he almost influenced everybody, as were Tex Avery and Bob Clampett. Robert Crumb was a big influence. Saul Steinberg.

Charles Addams, you know, the *Addams Family* guy? He was a big influence because his pictures were very dark and sick. He made fun of people dying, he made light of death, and I thought that was a real refreshing move. I mean, no one had ever done that so much before him, using people's pain and death as a source of humor.

A.B. Frost, who was a turn-of-the-century cartoonist. A great artist from Buenos Aires called Carlos Nine. Roland Topor, from France. Of course, the Beatles. Quentin Tarantino. Frank Capra. Let's see, who else? Tommy Ungerer is a big influence. Richard Lester, the British filmmaker who did the early Beatles films. Miyazaki. John Lasseter. Another big one was Preston Blair, who wrote the book *Animation*. Milt Kahl. You know, it goes on and on.

Considering how much light and dark is in your work—the sweet and the sour—do you see life as essentially a comedy, or a tragedy? I'm a very optimistic guy. Even as old as I am, it's weird, I'm very Pollyanna-ish. Oh, yeah, life is pleasure, totally. I was just walking down the street wondering how cool things are, just looking at people on the street and letting my imagination run wild. It's definitely a pleasure.

But some of my films are very violent, and they're not necessarily sad, but I certainly find a lot of humor in violence. And that, again, goes back to the Tex Avery cartoons, or the Charles Addams cartoons, and that it's sometimes good to laugh at our misfortune, or other people's misfortune. I don't know why, but when someone hits himself in the head with a rock or something, people laugh. I don't know the psychology of that, but it's funny.

I've heard it said that, quite simply, we laugh because it's not us. That could be, but I've made stupid blunders and hurt myself badly, and I've laughed at how stupid I am. So, I think it goes beyond that.

What's the weirdest thing you've ever seen or experienced? We were in the streets of New York, on the very first day of shooting *J. Lyle*, one of my live-action feature films. It was like a Sunday morning, a beautiful sunny day. This transvestite, basically naked except for a little negligee, started following me around the set and tipped over the craft services table, and attacked one of the crew with some scissors. So I grabbed this big roll of tar paper and started to sword fight, sort of like Errol Flynn and Basil Rathbone, trying to get this guy away from everybody. He stabbed me in the arm with the scissors. The cops came and the ambulance came and they hauled him away. He stabbed one of the cops, it was a real fracas. I just realized that when I'm doing animation, in my apartment, this never happens. It's much safer there.

Is there a question you've always wanted to answer, but no one's asked it yet? Yeah, there is a question I think interviewers should ask, and they rarely do: "Why do you do what you do?" Obviously, I could make more money if I was in the stock market, or a salesman or something like that. So, why do I do it? Because everybody has a different reason why they create, why they make their films. And I think it just started when I was a little kid, and I started to draw a lot. I just felt like there was a certain power in drawing something—whether it's a car or a pretty girl or a beautiful tree or something like that—there's a certain power you that have when you draw when

you draw these things, that you own them, that they become yours. Like, if I see a beautiful woman on the street and I draw that woman, I almost feel like I've had sex with her, because I control her. I created her. And I think that's one of the reasons that I love doing cartoons. It's a god-like feeling. It's a very all-powerful feeling. I guess it can go back to that whole totem thing of tribal societies, where they would do a totem of their god—or their rival tribe's, and they would stick pins in it and that sort of thing. There's a certain power in creating these characters in my film, that I own them, I control them. And I think that's one of the real reasons why I make these films.

Well, it's a good thing that you're a benevolent god watching over them. Yes, that is true. [*Laughter*] That is true. ☺

HOT DOG; IDIOTS AND ANGELS

MORE INFO
www.IdiotsAndAngels.com
www.Plymptoons.com

EXCERPT | Chapter One of a New Steampunk Novel

IT IS A WORLD OF GARGOYLES, AUTOMATA & INDUSTRIAL
REVOLUTIONARIES. IT IS **EKATERINA SEDIA'S**

The ALCHEMY of STONE

WE SCALE THE *rough bricks of the building's facade. Their crumbling edges soften under our claw-like fingers; they jut out of the flat, adenoid face of the wall to provide easy footholds. We could've used fire escapes, we could've climbed up, up, past the indifferent faces of the walls, their windows cataracted with shutters; we could've bounded up in the joyful cacophony of corrugated metal and barely audible whispers of the falling rust shaken loose by our ascent. We could've flown.*

But instead we hug the wall, press our cheeks against the warm bricks; the filigree of age and weather covering their surface imprints on our skin, steely-gray like the thunderous skies above us. We rest, clinging to the wall, our fingertips nestled in snug depressions in the brick, like they were made especially for that, clinging. We are almost all the way to the steep roof red with shingles shaped like fish scales.

We look into the lone window lit with a warm glow, the only one with open shutters and smells of sage, lamb and chlorine wafting outside. We look at the long bench decorated with alembics and retorts and colored powders and bunches of dried herbs and bowls of watery sheep's eyes from the butcher shop down the alleyway. We look at the girl.

Her porcelain face has cracked—a recent fall, an accident?—and we worry as we count the cracks cobwebbing her cheek and her forehead, radiating from the point of impact like sunrays. Yes, we remember the sun. Her blue eyes, facets of expensive glass colored

with copper salts, look into the darkness and we do not know if she can see us at all.

But she smiles and waves at us, and the bronzed wheel-bearings of her joints squeak their mechanical greeting. She pushes the lock of dark, dark hair (she doesn't know, but it used to belong to a dead boy) behind her delicate ear, a perfect and pink seashell. Her deft hands, designed for grinding and mixing and measuring, smooth the front of her fashionably wide skirt, and she motions to us. "Come in," she says.

We creep inside through the window, grudgingly, gingerly, we creep (we could've flown). We grow aware of our not-belonging, of the grayness of our skin, of our stench—we smell like pigeon-shit, and we wonder if she notices; we fill her entire room with our rough awkward sour bodies. "We seek your help," we say.

Her cracked porcelain face remains as expressionless as ours. "I am honored," she says. Her blue eyes bulge a little from their sockets, taking us in. Her frame clicks as she leans forward, curious about us. Her dress is low cut, and we see that there is a small transparent window in her chest, where a clockwork heart is ticking along steadily, and we cannot help but feel resentful of the sound and—by extension—of her, the sound of time falling away grain by grain, the time that dulls our senses and hardens our skins, the time that is in too short supply. "I will do everything I can," she says, and our resentment falls away too, giving way to gratitude; falls like dead skin. We bow and leap out of the window, one by one by one, and we fly, hopeful for the first time in centuries.

* * *

LOHARRI'S ROOM SMELLED of incense and smoke, the air thick like taffy. Mattie tasted it on her lips, and squinted through the thick haze concealing its denizen.

"Mattie," Loharri said from the chaise by the fireplace where he sprawled in his habitual languor, a half-empty glass on the floor. A fat black cat sniffed at its contents prissily, found them not to her liking, but knocked the glass over nonetheless, adding the smell of flat beer to the already overwhelming concoction that was barely air. "So glad to see you."

"You should open the window," she said.

"You don't need air," Loharri said, petulant. He was in one of his moods again.

"But you do," she pointed out. "You are one fart away from death by suffocation. Fresh air won't kill you."

"It might," he said, still sulking.

"Only one way to find out." She glided past him, the whirring of her gears muffled by the room—it was so full of draperies and old rugs rolled up in the corners, so cluttered with bits of machinery and empty dishes. Mattie reached up and swung open the shutters, admitting a wave of air sweet with lilac blooms and rich river mud and roasted nuts from the market square down the street. "Alive still?"

"Just barely." Loharri sat up and stretched, his long spine crackling like flywheels. He then yawned, his mouth gaping dark in his pale face. "What brings you here, my dear love?"

She extended her hand, the slender copper springs of her fingers grasping a phial of blue glass. "One of your admirers sent for me—she said you were ailing. I made you a potion."

Loharri uncorked the phial and sniffed at the contents with suspicion. "A woman? Which one?" he asked. "Because if it was a jilted lover, I am not drinking this."

"Amelia," Mattie said. "I do not suppose she wishes you dead."

"Not yet," Loharri said darkly, and drank. "What does it do?"

"Not yet," Mattie agreed. "It's just a tonic. It'll dispel your ennui, although I imagine a fresh breeze might do just as well."

Loharri made a face; he was not a hand-

some man to begin with, and a grimace of disgust did not improve his appearance.

Mattie smiled. "If an angel passes over you, your face will be stuck like that."

Loharri scoffed. "Dear love, if only it could make matters worse. But speaking of faces . . . yours has been bothering me lately. What did you do to it?"

Mattie touched the cracks, feeling their familiar swelling on the smooth porcelain surface. "Accident," she said.

Loharri arched his left eyebrow—the right one was paralyzed by the scar and the knotted mottled tissue that ruined half of his face; it was a miracle his eye had been spared. Mattie heard that some women found scars attractive in a romantic sort of way, but she was pretty certain that Loharri's were quite a long way past romantic and into disfiguring. "Another accident," he said. "You are a very clumsy automaton, do you know that?"

"I am not clumsy," Mattie said. "Not with my hands."

He scowled at the phial in his hand. "I guess not, although my taste buds beg to differ. Still, I made you a little something."

"A new face," Mattie guessed.

Loharri smiled lopsidedly and stood, and stretched his long, lanky frame again. He searched through the cluttered room until he came upon a workbench that somehow got hidden and lost under the pile of springs, coils, wood shavings, and half-finished suits of armor that appeared decorative rather than functional in their coppery, glistening glory. There were cogs and parts of engines and things that seemed neither animate nor entirely dead, and for a short while Mattie worried that the chaotic pile would consume Loharri; however, he soon emerged with a triumphant cry, a round white object in his hand.

It looked like a mask and Mattie averted her eyes—she did not like looking at her faces like that, as they hovered, blind and disembodied. She closed her eyes and extended her neck toward Loharri in a habitual gesture. His strong practiced fingers brushed the hair from her forehead, lingering just a sec-

ond too long, and felt around her jaw line, looking for the tiny cogs and pistons that attached her face to the rest of her head. She felt her face pop off, and the brief moment when she felt exposed, naked, seemed to last an eternity. She whirred her relief when she felt the touch of the new concave surface as it enveloped her, hid her from the world.

Loharri affixed the new face in place, and she opened her eyes. Her eyes took a moment to adjust to the new sockets.

"How does it fit?" Loharri asked.

"Well enough," she said. "Let me see how I look." She extended one of the flexible joints that held her eyes and tilted it, to see the white porcelain mask. Loharri had not painted this one—he remembered her complaints about the previous face, that it was too bright, too garish (this is why she broke it in the first place), and he left this one plain, suffused with the natural bluish tint that reminded her of the pale skies over the city during July and its heat spells. Only the lips, lined with pitted smell and taste sensors, were tinted pale red, same as the rooftops in the merchants' district.

"It is nice," Mattie said. "Thank you."

Loharri nodded. "Don't mention it. No matter how emancipated, you're still mine." His voice lost its usual acidity as he studied her new face with a serious expression. There were things Mattie and Loharri didn't talk about—one of them was Mattie's features, which remained constant from one mask to the next, no matter how much he experimented with colors and other elaborations. "Looks good," he finally concluded. "Now, tell me the real reason for your visit—surely, you don't rush over every time someone tells you I might be ill."

"The gargoyles," Mattie said. "They want to hire me, and I want your permission to make them my priority, at the expense of your project."

Loharri nodded. "It's a good one," he said. "I guess our gray overlords have grown tired of being turned into stone?"

"Yes," Mattie answered. "They feel that their life spans are too short and their fate is too cruel; I cannot say that I disagree. Only . . . I really do not know where to start. I thought of vitality potions and the mixes to soften the leather, of the elixirs to loosen the calcified joints . . . only they all seem lacking."

Loharri smiled and drummed his fingers on his knee. "I see your problem, and yes, you can work on it to your little clockwork heart's content."

"Thank you," Mattie said. If she had been able to smile, she would have. "I brought you what I have so far—a list of chemicals that change color when exposed to light."

Loharri took the proffered piece of paper with two long fingers, and opened it absent-mindedly. "I know little of alchemy," he said. "I'm not friends with any of your colleagues, but I suppose I could find a replacement for you nonetheless, although I doubt there's anyone who knows more on the matter than you do. Meanwhile, I do have one bit of advice regarding the gargoyles."

Mattie tilted her head to the shoulder, expectant. She had learned expressive poses, and knew that they amused her creator; she wondered if she was supposed to feel shame at being manipulative.

As expected, he snickered. "Aren't you just the sweetest machine in the city? And oh, you listen so well. Heed my words then: I remember a woman who worked on the gargoyle problem some years back. Beresta was her name, a foreigner; Beresta from the eastern district. But she died—a sad, sad thing."

"Oh," Mattie said, disappointed. "Did she leave any papers behind?"

Loharri shook his head. "No papers. But, lucky for you, she was a restless spirit, a sneaky little ghost who hid in the rafters of her old home. And you know what they do with naughty ghosts."

Mattie inclined her head in agreement. "They call for the Soul-Smoker."

"Indeed. And if there's anyone who still knows Beresta's secrets, it's him. You're not afraid of the Soul-Smokers, are you?"

"Of course not," Mattie said mildly. "I have no soul; to fear him would be a mere superstition." She stood and smoothed her

skirts, feeling the stiff whalebone stays that held her skirts full and round under the thin fabric. "Thank you, Loharri. You've been kind."

"Thank you for the tonic," he said. "But please, do visit me occasionally, even if there's nothing you want. I am a sentimental man."

"I shall," Mattie answered, and took her leave. As she walked out of the door, it occurred to her that if she wanted to be kind to Loharri she could offer him things she knew he wanted but would never ask for—she could invite him to touch her hair, or let him listen to the ticking of her heart. To sit with him in the darkness, in the dead hours between night and morning when the demons tormented him more than usual, and then perhaps he would talk of things they did not talk about otherwise—perhaps then he would tell her why he had made her and why he grew so despondent when she wanted to live on her own and to study, to become something other than a part of him. The problem was, those were the things she preferred not to know.

MATTIE TOOK A long way home, weaving through the market among the many stalls selling food and fabric and spices; she lingered by a booth that sold imported herbs and chemicals, and picked up a bunch of dried salamanders and a bottle of copper salts. She then continued east to the river, and she stood a while on the embankment watching the steamboats huff across, carrying marble for the new construction on the northern bank. There were talks of the new parliament building, and Mattie supposed that it signaled an even bigger change than gossip at Loharri's parties suggested. Ever since the mechanics won a majority, the renovations in the city acquired a feverish pace, and the streets themselves seemed to shift daily, accommodating new roads and more and more factories that belched smoke and steam and manufactured new and frightening machines.

Still, Mattie tried not to think of politics too much. She thought about gargoyles and

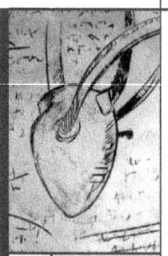

of Loharri's words. He called them their overlords, even though the city owed its existence to the gargoyles, and they had been nothing but benefactors to the people. Did he know something she didn't? And if he were so disdainful of gargoyles, why did he offer to help?

Mattie walked leisurely along the river. It was a nice day, and many people strolled along the embankment, enjoying the first spring warmth and the sweet dank smell of the river. She received a few curious looks, but overall people paid her no mind. She passed a paper factory that squatted over the river like an ugly toad, disgorging a stream of white foam into the water; a strong smell of bleach surrounded it like a cloud.

From the factory she turned into the twisty streets of the eastern district, where narrow three-storied buildings clung close together like swallows' nests on the face of a cliff. The sea of red tiled roofs flowed and ebbed as far as the eye could see, and Mattie smiled—she liked her neighborhood the way it was, full of people and small shops occupying the lower stories, without any factories and with the streets too narrow for any mechanized conveyances. She turned into her street and headed home, the ticking of her heart keeping pace with her thoughts filled with gargoyles and Loharri's strange relationship to them.

Mattie's room and laboratory were located above an apothecary's, which she occasionally supplied with elixirs and ointments. Less mainstream remedies remained in her laboratory, and those who sought them knew to visit her rooms upstairs; they usually used the back entrance and rickety stairs that led past the apothecary.

When Mattie got home to her garret, she found a visitor waiting on the steps. She had met this woman before at one of Loharri's gatherings—her name was Iolanda; she stood out from the crowd, Mattie remembered—she moved energetically and laughed loudly, and looked Mattie straight in the eye when they were introduced. And now Iolanda's gaze did not waver. "May I come in?" she said as soon as she saw Mattie, and smiled.

"Of course," Mattie said and unlocked the door. The corridor was narrow and led directly into her room that contained a roll top desk and her few books; Mattie led her visitor through and into the laboratory, where there was space to sit and talk.

"Would you like a drink?" Mattie asked. "I have a lovely jasmine-flavored liqueur."

Iolanda nodded. "I would love that. How considerate of you to keep refreshments."

Mattie poured her a drink. "Of course," she said. "How kind of you to notice."

Iolanda took the proffered glass from Mattie's copper fingers, studying them as she did so, and took a long swallow. "Indeed, it is divine," she said. "Now, if you don't mind, I would like to dispense with the pleasantries and state my business."

Mattie inclined her head and sat on a stool by her workbench, offering the other one to Iolanda with a gesture.

"You are not wealthy," Iolanda said. Not a question but a statement.

"Not really," Mattie agreed. "But I do not need much."

"Mmmm," Iolanda said. "One might suspect that a well-off alchemist is a successful alchemist—you do need to buy your ingredients, and some are more expensive than others."

"That is true," Mattie said. "Now, how does this relate to your business?"

"I can make you rich," Iolanda said. "I have need of an alchemist, of one who is discreet and skillful. But before I explain my needs, let me ask you this: do you consider yourself a woman?"

"Of course," Mattie said, taken aback and puzzled. "What else would I consider myself?"

"Perhaps I did not phrase it well," Iolanda said, and tossed back the remainder of her drink with an unexpectedly habitual and abrupt gesture. "What I meant was, why do you consider yourself a woman? Because you were created as one?"

"Yes," Mattie replied although she grew increasingly uncomfortable with the conversation. "And because of the clothes I wear."

"So if you changed your clothes . . ."

"But I can't," Mattie said. "The shape of them is built into me—I know that you have to wear corsets and hoops and stays to give your clothes a proper shape. But I was created with all of those already in place, they are as much as part of me as my eyes. So I ask you: what else would you consider me?"

"I sought not to offend," Iolanda said. "I do confess to my prejudice: I will not do business nor would I employ a person or an automaton of a gender different from mine, and I simply had to know if your gender was coincidental."

"I understand," Mattie said. "And I assure you that my femaleness is as ingrained as your own."

Iolanda sighed. Mattie supposed that Iolanda was beautiful, with her shining dark curls cascading onto her full shoulders and chest, and heavy languid eyelids half-concealing her dark eyes. "Fair enough. And Loharri . . . can you keep secrets from him?"

"I can and I do," Mattie said.

"In this case, I will appreciate it if you keep our business private," Iolanda said.

"I will, once you tell me what it is," Mattie replied. She shot an involuntary look toward her bench, where the ingredients waited for her to grind and mix and vaporize them, where the aludel yawned empty as if hungry; she grew restless sitting for too long empty-handed and motionless.

Iolanda raised her eyebrows, as if unsure whether she understood Mattie. She seemed one of those people who rarely encountered anything but abject agreement, and she was not used to being hurried. "Well, I want you to be available for the times I have a need of you, and to fulfill my orders on a short notice. Potions, perfumes, tonics . . . that sort of thing. I will pay you a retainer, so you will be receiving money even when I do not have a need of you."

"I have other clients and projects," Mattie said.

Iolanda waved her hand dismissively. "It doesn't matter. As long as I can find you when I need you."

"It sounds reasonable," Mattie agreed. "I will endeavor to fulfill simple orders within a

day, and complex ones—from two days to a week. You won't have them done faster anywhere."

"It is acceptable," Iolanda said. "And for your first order, I need you to create me a fragrance that would cause regret."

"Come back tomorrow," Mattie said. "Or leave me your address, I'll have a courier bring it over."

"No need," Iolanda said. "I will send someone to pick it up. And here's your first week's pay." She rose from her stool and placed a small pouch of stones on the bench. "And if anyone asks, we are casual acquaintances, nothing more."

Iolanda left, and Mattie felt too preoccupied to even look at the stones that were her payment. She almost regretted agreeing to Iolanda's requests—while they seemed straightforward and it was not that uncommon for courtiers to employ alchemists or any other artisans on a contract basis, something about Iolanda seemed off. Most puzzling, if she wanted to keep a secret from Loharri, she could do better than hire the automaton made by his hands. Mattie was not so vain as to presuppose that her reputation outweighed common good sense.

But there was work to do, and perfume certainly seemed less daunting than granting gargoyles a lifespan extension, and she mixed ambergris and sage, blended myrrh and the bark of grave cypress, and sublimated dry camphor. The smell she obtained was pleasing and sad, and yet she was not certain that this was enough to evoke regret—something seemed missing. She closed her eyes and smelled-tasted the mixture with her sensors, trying hard to remember the last time she felt regret. ☯

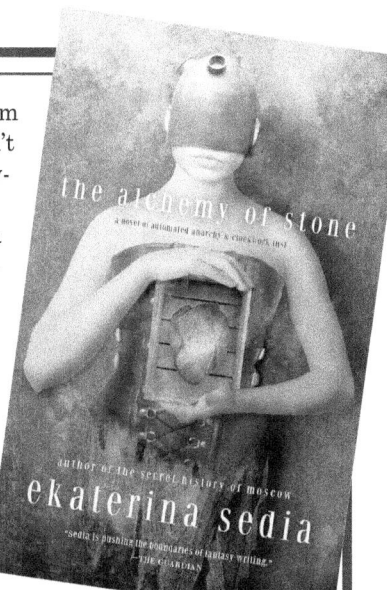

READ MORE!

THE ALCHEMY OF STONE by Ekaterina Sedia
Prime Books, trade paperback, $12.95 | On sale now
More info: www.ekaterinasedia.com

Ekaterina Sedia is the author of *The Secret History of Moscow*. A native of Russia, she lives in New Jersey.

Lost in Lovecraft

A GUIDED TOUR OF THE DARK MASTER'S WORLD

BY KENNETH HITE

"*It was in one of the most open and least frequented parts of the broad Pacific that the packet of which I was supercargo fell a victim to the German sea-raider.*"
— H.P. Lovecraft, "Dagon"

FOR A NEW ENGLANDER, Lovecraft gives surprisingly short shrift to the Atlantic. "The Temple" and a few minor pieces aside, almost all of Lovecraft's oceanic brooding concerns the vast Pacific. The Pacific swells in "Dagon," HPL's first story in *Weird Tales*, and if we take Australia as a Pacific nation, its waves are audible in "The Shadow Out of Time," his penultimate tale. So what surfaces in Lovecraft, in the "least frequented parts" of the ocean?

"*With the upheaval of new land in the South Pacific tremendous events began.*"
— H.P. Lovecraft,
At the Mountains of Madness

As befits our subject, let's broaden the scope somewhat. To Americans, even to New Englanders, the Pacific has long been the next frontier. When America's westward expansion hit the shores of California and Oregon, it kept going: to Hawaii and Samoa and Guam and the Philippines in Lovecraft's youth. Lovecraft's fellow Yankees started "the China trade" in 1790, furs and then whale oil and sandalwood across the Pacific to Canton, and it made them rich. Like the "amber waves of grain" in the West, the Pacific is a treasure-house. Melville, for example, repeatedly equates Pacific whales and gold in *Moby-Dick*, reinforcing the parallel to the agrarian West with "harvest" metaphors. Lovecraft intriguingly recasts the image: in "The Shadow Over Innsmouth," Obed Marsh finds actual gold in the Pacific and brings it back to Innsmouth—along with the Pacific's Deep One taint.

* * *

"*He was the only one as kep' on with the East-Injy an' Pacific trade, though Esdras Martin's barkentine Malay Bride made a venter as late as twenty-eight.*"
— H.P. Lovecraft, "The Shadow Over Innsmouth"

Here Lovecraft and Innsmouth wash up against the other great American trope of the Pacific: as a lure for Americans, a prelapsarian paradise of indolent lotus-eating. Melville's *Typee* and *Omoo* portray castaways or marooned victims worrying about being absorbed by the Pacific, or rather, by the Pacific islanders' alien culture. James Fenimore Cooper's *The Crater* mirrors this metaphor: an idyllic Pacific island actually sinks under the weight of too many modern Americans. Jack London's *South Seas Tales* likewise present the Pacific as an all-too-seductive beauty spot, remote from the modern world. (Outside America, Paul Gaugin and Robert Louis Stevenson, among others, do their best to reinforce this vision.) While Lovecraft writes no paeans to the glories of Tahiti, note the siren calls in his Innsmouth ship names: *Malay Bride* and *Sumatra Queen*. Arch hints at the nature of the "Innsmouth taint" to be sure, but also evidence of the Pacific's powers of seduction. In *Moby-Dick*, Melville sets it out: "Lifted by those eternal swells, you needs must own the seductive god, bowing your head to Pan," and his story is of a man driven mad by a seductive god, a sea-monster from the Pacific.

"*I talked with the mind of Yiang-Li, a philosopher from the cruel empire of Tsan-Chan, which is to come in 5,000 A.D. . . . with that of an archimage of vanished Yhe in the Pacific . . .*"
— H.P. Lovecraft, "The Shadow Out of Time"

If the Pacific washes away the rational and modern, it does so not least because the Pacific is ancient, its people seen as still the "noble savages" of Enlightenment prehistory, each of its islands an antediluvian

> *The Pacific is simultaneously unthinkably ancient and looming in the future, both long-dead and stirring to be born.*

Eden. But in keeping with our earlier frontier trope, the Pacific is also the future. (Even now, one can hear that the 21st will be the "Pacific Century," as history zooms westward around the globe.) So, better yet, the Pacific is not merely ancient, but timeless. Again in *Moby-Dick*, Melville notes that the Pacific waves wash "the new-built Californian towns, but yesterday planted by the recentest race of men, and lave the faded but still gorgeous skirts of Asiatic lands, older than Abraham."

Lovecraft finds this metaphor of timelessness far more congenial than the "island Eden" trope. The Pacific is simultaneously unthinkably ancient and looming in the future, both long-dead and stirring to be born. Lovecraft's cosmic sensibilities thrill to the duality. His "Dagon" is both an ancient god and a modern threat. The "Kanakys" wiped out the Deep Ones off Othaheite, but their race plans its resurgence—"the reel horror . . . ain't what them fish devils hez done, but what they're a-goin' to do!"—in Pacific-tainted Innsmouth. In "The Shadow Out of Time," the catalogue of entities met by Nathaniel Peaslee includes representatives of both distant past and future Pacifics: Yhe and Tsan-Chan. Lovecraft's ultimate blending of the timeless, the primordial, the apocalyptic, and the Pacific looms over them all: Great Cthulhu.

"Remains of Them, he said the deathless Chinamen had told him, were still to be found as Cyclopean stones on islands in the Pacific."
                —H.P. Lovecraft, "The Call of Cthulhu"

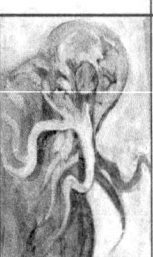

Cthulhu is very much of the Pacific, even of a specific spot therein, somewhere between Pitcairn Island (where the *Bounty* mutineers succumbed to the Pacific's seductions) and Easter Island (with its "ancient" statues). Even Cthulhu has perhaps bowed his head to Pan; his Pacific "deep waters" are "full of the one primal mystery through which not even thought can pass." But Cthulhu also is Pan, "the madness from the sea." Cthulhu is a prehistoric memory and the inevitable future all in one, both old and new, as Wilcox notes of his bas-relief at the beginning of the story: "It is new, indeed, for I made it last night in a dream of strange cities; and dreams are older than brooding Tyre, or the contemplative Sphinx." Cthulhu once ruled the Earth, then fell in a cataclysm, but "when the stars come right" he will emerge again in a kind of parodic Last Judgment, "a glorious resurrection...a holocaust of ecstasy."

This rhythm, of ancient greatness, catastrophic destruction, current desuetude, and future ascension at the end of the age, is the rhythm of Theosophy. So Lovecraft slyly acknowledges in the introduction to "The Call of Cthulhu": "Theosophists have guessed at the awesome grandeur of the cosmic cycle... [and] have hinted at strange survival in terms which would freeze the blood if not masked by a bland optimism." Lovecraft wrote "Cthulhu" shortly after reading a Theosophical omnibus, *The Story of Atlantis and the Lost Lemuria* by William Scott-Elliot, and specifically mentions that tome in the tale as one of Angell's "Cthulhu Cult" file sources. No one will be surprised to see Pacific mega-continents, sunken islands, and prehuman survivals prominently featured in Scott-Elliot's pages, albeit "masked by a bland optimism." Lovecraft further "demythologizes" Theosophy, recasting it as paleontology in *At the Mountains of Madness*, as the bas-reliefs in Kadath tell the epoch-spanning tale of prehuman races and sunken lands in the Pacific.

* * *

"Centuries hence ... China may yet form a titanic world force to be reckoned with. It would be curious if the oldest of all civilisations of today were to survive its younger rivals in the end."
—H.P. Lovecraft, letter to Henry George Weiss (Feb. 3, 1937)

Shrinking our scope down a bit from prehuman ecologies to mere lost civilizations, another beat of the Theosophist rhythm is that India, or "Asia," was great before the West was born, and would rise again to reduce Europe to irrelevance. (Lovecraft's fellow New Englander Emerson said much the same thing.) This fed not only Indian nationalism, but paradoxically fueled Western racism. The generally hopeful message of Theosophy is essentially identical to the generally fearful message of "the Yellow Peril": the dreaming, even sessile "Asiatics" (for Lovecraft and Americans, on the other side of the Pacific) will awaken from their slumber and destroy the (white) world. Sound familiar?

Lovecraft invokes the Yellow Peril even before he reads Theosophy: in "Polaris," "He," and "Nyarlathotep," the future is yellow, and (white) civilization is overthrown. When he adds Theosophy to the mixture, things get even weirder: in the cosmic time-cycles of "Through the Gates of the Silver Key," HPL takes time to note that Pickman Carter "in

Cthulhu is very much of the Pacific — even of a specific spot therein, between Pitcairn and Easter Islands.

the year 2169 would use strange means in repelling the Mongol hordes from Australia," and we've already met "the cruel empire of Tsan-Chan" of 5000 A.D. Lovecraft doesn't leave the Yellow Peril in his fiction, either. In a 1919 letter to Alfred Galpin and Maurice Moe, he predicts that the Chinese "are a menace of the still more distant future" who "will probably be the exterminators of Caucasian civilization." And in a 1934 letter to Natalie Wooley, only the specifics change: "In the end—as we grow weak & decadent ... Japan will probably dominate the world," but HPL hopes "that period will be thousands of years in the future." It's not just Theosophy, then, that leads Lovecraft to put "deathless Chinamen" in charge of the Cthulhu Cult.

"The West, however, was never favourable to [the Ghatanothoa cult's] growth ... In the end it became a hunted, doubly furtive underground affair—yet never could its nucleus be quite exterminated. It always survived somehow, chiefly in the Far East and on the Pacific Islands, where its teachings became merged into the esoteric lore of the Polynesian Areoi."

—H.P. Lovecraft and Hazel Heald, "Out of the Aeons"

Is "Call of Cthulhu" just a strange Yellow Peril story, Fu Manchu with tentacles? No, it's far vaster than that; it partakes not just of Theosophy's Pacific apocalypses, but the iconic Pacifics of Jack London and Herman Melville: forgetfulness and timelessness, madness and obsession. But for Lovecraft, at least, the Pacific is inextricable from the shores it washes. He demonstrates this in "Out of the Aeons," as the survivors of the lost continent of Mu (Lemuria renamed by a different Theosophist crackpot, Colonel Churchward) gather in pilgrimage before the mummy of Tyog. By the time the story is done, the litany of "swarthy Asiatics" and "eccentric foreigners" has included Hawaiians, Ceylonese, Filipinos, Peruvian Indians, East Indians, Burmese, and Fijians—and Lovecraft's own authorial stand-in, Randolph Carter, in his "Swami Chandraputra" garb from "Through the Gates of the Silver Key." The Pacific swallows Lovecraft, too; he has bowed his head before the seductive god Pan. Or Dagon. Or Cthulhu. ☉

Next Stop on the Tour: *New York City*